DEEP AMBER

C. J. Busby

templar

A TEMPLAR BOOK

First published in the UK in 2014 by Templar Publishing,

an imprint of The Templar Company Limited,

Deepdene Lodge, Deepdene Avenue, Dorking, Surrey,

RH5 4AT, UK

www.templarco.co.uk

Text copyright © 2014 by C. J. Busby

Illustrations copyright © 2014 by David Wyatt

First UK edition

ISBN 978-1-84877-603-6

Printed and bound in Great Britain by

CPI Group (UK) Ltd, Croydon, CR0 4YY

For Dad, the original Forest Agent

Chapter One

It was Dora who discovered the first of the strange objects. She put her foot on it as she hurried down the turret stairs and slipped, and together she and the strange object bumped all the way down the steps to the bottom. She landed upside down right in front of Sir Roderick, who looked at her disapprovingly down his long nose.

"Umm… Sorry!" stuttered Dora, hurriedly getting herself the right way up. She felt around for the object that had sent her flying and discovered the oddest pair of spectacles she had ever seen. They were made of some kind of soft, dark metal that was completely bendy, like someone had taken a pair of spectacles and melted them in a cauldron. But they weren't at all hot, they were cool and slimy to the touch, and instead of straight arms that sat on your ears they had a band of the soft metal that went right round your head.

Cautiously, she tried them on… and then whipped them straight off again. The eye part had sucked itself right onto her face, like a sea-creature clinging to a rock. It felt horrible. She decided she'd better take them to the Druid.

The Druid was generally to be found down in the castle cellars, with his cauldrons, spells and potions. This meant Dora would have to cross the yard to get to him. As she reached the arched doorway out of the turret, Dora hesitated. The yard appeared to be empty. But as she slipped out, she heard a cackling burst of laughter and saw Violet Wetherby, the cook's daughter, sweep into the yard towing her friends behind her like a gaggle of hens. When they saw Dora, they stopped, and nudged each other. Then they all sauntered over, spreading out so that she was forced to walk through the middle of the group.

"Well, if it isn't little Dora Puddlefoot," said Violet in a mocking voice, one eyebrow raised. "Out in the sunshine for once, instead of hiding in a dark cellar. And how are you today, Dora? Broken anything lately? Fallen over your own feet again? You must be careful not to *really* hurt yourself, you know. We all love having you around. It's *so* much fun…"

The other girls laughed, and jostled Dora as she passed. She could feel their mocking glances burning into her back as she continued across the yard.

Violet was eleven, the same age as Dora, but she acted older, flirting with all the squires, and queening it over her little troop of allies. When Dora had arrived six months ago as the new apprentice witch, Violet had taken an instant dislike to her, and when Violet took a dislike to anyone, so did all her gang.

Dora thought – for the hundredth time – about putting a really horrible spell on Violet Wetherby. She could turn her golden hair into slugs, and make sure she smelled of rotten eggs for a week. But Dora knew she wouldn't do it. She was too anxious about getting into trouble for misusing her magic and being sent back to her village in disgrace.

As Dora clattered down the cellar stairs, the Druid was bent over, frowning at the mixture in his cauldron. Pushing his messy black hair out of his eyes, he looked up from his potion making. Normally, he was glad to see his timid young apprentice. She had considerably more magic than any of his previous students, and teaching her spells was an entertaining affair. Her magic was extremely powerful but just a little bit wonky – so her potions might turn their user blue, or make the cauldron explode. The Druid quite liked the unexpectedness of this. It made life more fun.

Today, however, he was cooking up a very difficult spell for repelling dragons. He had reached a delicate stage, and the last thing he wanted at this moment was Dora's sideways magic finding its way into the potion.

"Out, out, out!" he bellowed as she slipped into the cellar. He flapped his hands at her. "I can't have you ruin this – it's in the final stages! Come back tomorrow! Or better still – next Tuesday!"

Dora came to an abrupt halt, a little worry line appearing between her eyebrows, but she stood her ground. Carefully she held out the strange spectacles so the Druid could see them clearly.

Immediately he stopped his flapping and

stood very still, looking at the object in her hands. For a second he closed his eyes, and sighed deeply. Then he opened his eyes, came over to where she was standing at the bottom of the stairs, and reached out for the strange spectacles. He looked down at them, lying all floppy in his large brown hands.

"Goggles," he said.

"What?" said Dora.

"Swimming goggles. For going under water. Where did you find them?"

"On the turret stairs," said Dora. "Did you say water?"

The Druid looked at her and smiled, but his clear brown eyes looked strangely sad. "Yes, water. They're for seeing under the surface."

"Are they magic?" said Dora, but she already knew they didn't feel in the least bit magical – just shiny and odd and a bit frightening.

"No," said the Druid. "Not magic. Here – I'll show you."

He snapped the goggles onto Dora's head, and she flinched as the slimy eye-pieces sucked onto her face. Then the Druid led her over to a large cauldron of water standing by the wall.

"Hold your breath," he ordered, and then pushed her face down into the cauldron.

Dora gasped and choked and flailed her arms but as she emerged dripping from the water she realised that she had seen the bottom of the cauldron while she was under. Curious, she bobbed her head back down. The strange sucking spectacles created a bubble of air close to her eyes, so she could easily keep them open. She looked around at the salt-encrusted sides of the cauldron, and spotted a couple of little fish that had got in by accident when the cauldron was filled with moat water. She almost forgot that she wasn't breathing, until the Druid yanked her out by one dark plait. She inhaled a whole lungful of air with a whoop and nearly fell over from the dizziness of it.

"Good, aren't they?' he said with a twinkle in his eye, and then shoved her back up the stairs. "Off you go – you can let everyone try them out… I've got work to do."

The goggles were the wonder of the castle for a week. The squires fought each other for the right to use them, and even a few of the knights had a go. Jem the kitchen boy scorned them to start with – he said he could see under the water anyway – but being able to see without getting bits of moat-grit in your eyes or your eyelids gummed together with slime was counted quite a triumph by everyone else. And when one of the squires found a gold necklace nestling in the weeds at the bottom of the castle duck pond, even Jem admitted they were probably the most useful strange object that had ever appeared in the castle.

But that was before they found the second one.

This time it was Lady Alys who found it, in her bedchamber. She decided it must be an odd kind of bracelet, since it hung from a short chain. But it was rather bulky for a piece of jewellery, and not very attractive – shiny enough, but square and black and heavy.

Dora was on the way to muck out the pigs when she saw Lady Alys's new bracelet. Strictly speaking, it wasn't her turn to do the pigs, but Lizzie, the blacksmith's daughter and Dora's only real friend in the castle, had agreed to swap pig duty for sewing. Sewing involved sitting in a turret room surrounded by Violet and her friends, and Dora had decided several weeks before that she preferred the company of the pigs.

"It was just on the floor, by the fireside," Lady Alys was explaining to the crowd around her. "I must have a secret admirer! Maybe Sir Bedwyr," she added hopefully, as she twirled the strange bracelet round. Sir Bedwyr was extremely handsome and quite the best swordsman in the castle, but as yet he hadn't declared his undying love to anyone.

Lady Rosamund, who also fancied her chances with the castle's most eligible knight, snorted.

"Not very likely, since he's been out hunting all day," she said scornfully. "Dora! You're good with magic. Come and have a look at this. Where's it come from?"

Dora came over cautiously. Lady Rosamund was blonde and blue-eyed and looked like a goddess, but she had a temper like a wildcat and although she seemed to like talking to Dora, Dora always felt a bit awkward around her.

She took the strange object in her hands, and knew at once that it was from the same place as the peculiar goggles. It felt equally odd, out of place and completely devoid of any magic. It was like a small box, with odd shapes carved into the sides, and shiny circular buttons. Dora shook it, and tried pressing one of the buttons. There was a noise like a cart rattling over cobblestones and a squat black tower rose out of the front of the box. Everyone jumped, and Dora nearly dropped it.

The short tower was shiny, and the end of it was oddly reflective, like looking into a dark pool of water. Dora held the box up, and peered into the end of the tower, and tried touching another button. The box made a sound like a pickaxe hitting a stone. Suddenly, on the other side of the box, a window seemed to click open. Dora turned the box round and looked at the window. Staring out from the other side in wonder was a tiny, frozen Dora, her mouth open in surprise.

Once they'd worked out how to make the little frozen pictures appear in the box, the whole castle exploded with the joy of capturing each other's noses, ears, feet and other bits in the box's dark window.

Lady Rosamund produced a perfect reflection of Lady Alys's nostrils and managed to show it to almost every knight in the castle before Lady

Alys wrestled her to the ground and forcibly removed the box from her wrist. And then Jem got hold of it, and that was that, because he was the fastest runner in the whole of the western borders. A succession of portraits of hairy warts, goggling eyes, cow's bottoms and worse were flashed in front of eager audiences before being whipped away and replaced with something even more undignified.

Lizzie joined Dora in the pigsty to report that Jem had even managed to get a picture of Sir Bedwyr in the privy.

"He's charging all the castle ladies a silver piece each to look at it," she giggled. "Sir Bedwyr's fuming!"

Finally, Jem froze an image of Sir Roderick falling off his horse. It was the last straw. Sir Roderick and Sir Mortimer cornered the kitchen boy and boxed his ears, and Dora was given the strange box to take to the Druid.

"Camera," said the Druid, when Dora brought it to him.

"I'm sorry?" said Dora, frowning.

"It's no good," he said, looking worried.

"Something is going to have to be done, before it all gets out of hand." He stood for a moment, frowning. "I'm not going," he muttered to himself. "I can't… I *promised*. It will have to be Ravenglass, or the forest. They'll have to deal with it."

Dora didn't have any idea what he was talking about, but that was quite normal with the Druid. She waited, while he ran his hands through his messy dark hair, thinking hard, and then sat down on a nearby bench. He gestured to Dora to sit beside him.

"Dora," he said encouragingly. "How would you feel about taking a message to the palace?"

Dora looked down at her feet. She didn't know quite what to say. On the one hand, the journey to the city was a long one and the thought of having to deliver an important message to the royal palace made Dora feel so nervous she thought she might be sick. But on the other hand, the chance of getting away from the castle – and Violet's gang – was very tempting.

"Um… I think I could do that," she said cautiously, looking up at the Druid. "What would the message be?"

The Druid turned the camera over in his

hands, and seemed to hesitate for a moment. He sighed.

"These objects come from another world," he said. "One I happen to know rather well, in fact. Now, it's not that unusual to get one coming through every now and again. But more than one thing at the same time, from the same world, is… rather odd. Possibly dangerous."

"They're from another world?" said Dora. How could there be another world? Other worlds were just things that you got in the old stories, from the time when the heroes had lived. They didn't really exist. And yet – when she thought of the goggles, and the strange camera box with its buttons and bright shiny blackness, she realised that they were like nothing she'd ever come across before – not to mention being completely empty of magic.

"Yes," said the Druid, handing her the camera and stretching out his long legs. "Another world. A whole other place, quite different from ours. Hardly anyone knows about the other worlds these days, but there are lots of them. Some have magic, some have plumbing." His voice sounded wistful.

Dora had no idea what plumbing was, but it sounded alarming.

"We need to send a message to the palace," the Druid continued, "and whoever takes it will have to go through the Great Forest – it's the quickest way. It could also be important that the forest folk are told about this as well. So I need a magic user. I can't really spare anyone else, and besides, you *did* find the goggles. Do you think you could manage it?"

"Through the forest?" Dora said, in a slightly shaky voice. "But it's…"

"Dangerous, deep and thoroughly enchanted," said the Druid. "I know. But it's not as bad as people make out, you know. The forest folk like to keep its reputation fearsome – it keeps the idiots out. But it'll be easy for a powerful magic user like you, Dora. They'll like you."

Dora couldn't help feeling pleased by the praise – and although going through the Great Forest and possibly meeting one of the magical forest folk was a scary prospect, it was also undoubtedly an adventure. Besides, the thought of Violet's face when she heard that Dora was to go to the palace was too satisfying to resist.

"Um… all right," she said, trying to make her voice sound confident. "I'll go."

The Druid looked down at her with a grin and patted her on the shoulder.

"Good, I was hoping you would. You have just the right sort of magic for dealing with the forest. But we'll have to send a companion with you – you are a bit young to go on your own."

He looked thoughtful.

"I'd send Sir Bedwyr, but he's heading off on a quest tomorrow," he mused. "Most of the other knights are busy with the Summer Fair preparations. And you need someone with a bit of cunning, really."

He pondered for a moment, and then clicked his fingers.

"I know! We'll send Jem with you!"

He brightened at the thought of getting rid of Jem for a week. But Dora looked horrified.

"No! Not Jem… Please! I can manage on my own, honestly!"

"Sorry," said the Druid happily. "Out of the question. Jem's as sharp as a needle, and handy with a sword as well. He'll make sure you get there safe and sound. Go and tell him to pack at once!"

Chapter Two

No one was particularly bothered when the swimming goggles went missing – things had a habit of disappearing in Great-Aunt Irene's rambling old house. Simon, his mum and his big sister Catrin had only moved there a few months ago, when Great-Aunt Irene died, but already they were used to things getting lost and then reappearing a few days later.

But when the camera disappeared it was different. Cat had been banking on being able to take her camera to photography club, and maybe have half a very slim chance of meeting someone she actually liked at the horrible school she'd been dragged to when they moved. So she was madder than a nest of hornets when she found her camera had gone.

"I left it here! In my bedroom! Only last night!" she stormed at Simon. "It can't just have gone! You must have moved it!"

Simon shrugged and raised one eyebrow, which just made her crosser than ever, and it wasn't long before she was slapping and he was kicking and their mum was shouting at them both.

"For goodness sake! It's just a camera! It'll turn up. It's probably under the bed," she said, exasperated.

But it wasn't under the bed, and it didn't turn up, and Cat was convinced Simon had lost it somewhere. In retaliation, she administered a few swift and secretive kicks in Simon's direction when their mum wasn't looking.

Simon was used to rough justice from his older sister, and ignored her. But it was hard for either of them to ignore what happened next.

Disappearing objects was one thing, but *appearing* objects was quite another. Especially when what appeared was a large and elaborately engraved sword.

Simon found it in the middle of the stairs when he came down for breakfast the next morning.

He nearly tripped over it, but stopped just in time. He was a bit bleary-eyed from a late night and strange dreams, so he had to blink a few times before he was sure it was real. But there it was – a long shining sword, lying on the stair-carpet. He crouched down and reached out to pick the sword up. It was heavy, and there was something about it that made his hands tingle – something like electricity, or the feeling you get when someone traces a feather down your arm.

He sat for a moment, just holding it, then continued down the stairs and put the sword carefully on the kitchen table next to his old red DS before getting himself a bowl of cornflakes.

"What the…? Where did you get *that*?" said Cat, who was sitting at the kitchen table, dressed in a sloppy jumper and pyjama bottoms, and on her second round of toast. It was Sunday, and Mum was out for the day. She'd left early for a conference on ancient Saxon grave goods and wouldn't be back till late, so they had the house to themselves. "Is it something Mum left behind?"

Simon frowned. "I don't think so. It's something very weird. It was in the middle of the stairs. Touch it – see what you think."

Cat reached out one hand and gingerly touched the sword. Instantly she drew her hand back.

"Urrghh! It's like it's alive or something. What *is* it?"

They looked at each other across the table. Cat ran her hands distractedly through her short blonde hair. At thirteen, she was two years older than Simon, and she was officially in charge on the days when Mum was away. Their dad had died when Simon was three, and since Mum did a lot of travelling to different conferences and archaeological digs and museums for work, they were quite used to having to fend for themselves. Cat was good at organising things and being bossy, and Simon was used to doing what she told him to, so things generally worked out just fine. But things didn't usually include a large sword appearing in the house without warning.

"You can't have found it on the stairs," she said with a frown. "There was nothing there when I came down earlier."

As they looked at each other, there was a sudden knock at the front door. Cat jumped. Simon carefully pulled the sword off the table and slid it underneath, on to his knees. He wasn't sure why he did this, but something about the sword made him feel very protective – he didn't want anyone else to see it until they'd had a chance to have a proper look at it.

There was another knock, sharp and imperious. Cat got up, and went to the door. Standing outside were two men dressed in shiny black suits. Both were tall and thin, but one was younger and glossier and the other more gaunt and somehow dusty.

"Ah, good morning," said the glossy one, in a nasal voice. He stretched his mouth into the semblance of a smile and nodded at her briskly. "The name's Smith – and this is Mr Jones." He gestured at the dusty man, whose face twitched briefly. *Only his eyes look in the least bit alive*, thought Cat, but as if to make up for the rest of him, they seemed more alive than was quite bearable.

"We're here from the National Radiological Protection Board," said Mr Smith, waving a laminated card in front of Cat's face. "We have reason to believe there may be a radiation leak in this area, so we're checking out all the homes at risk. It's quite routine. Just a precaution. So if you could just…?" He gestured into the house, and as Cat hesitated, gently inserted himself into the hallway.

"Thank you very much, Miss Arnold," he said, in his nasal voice. "If we could just take a few measurements around the house…"

Mr Smith set off down the hallway, his movements oddly jerky, his fingers brushing the walls as he passed as though he were trying to feel what was behind them. Mr Jones slid past Cat, holding his large briefcase in front of him, and walked stiffly after his companion. Cat, taken aback, wasn't sure what to do. Should she call the police? She hesitated, but it was already too late – the men had almost reached the kitchen and Simon was alone in there. She hurried down the corridor after them.

"Ah, good morning, young sir," said Mr Smith, as he walked into the kitchen and spotted Simon, frozen at the table. "Don't mind us, we're just checking the radiation levels. If you would, Mr Jones…?"

Mr Jones put the briefcase on the table very gently and his long white fingers moved rapidly over the complicated set of catches and locks. The briefcase sprang open and revealed a dull grey cube, with a number of dials and knobs, which appeared to be making a low humming noise.

Mr Jones made some adjustments to the dials and watched as various displays flickered and moved. As he observed them, his face hardly changed, but his strange bird-like eyes seemed to grow even brighter. Simon began to feel increasingly nervous. The sword on his knees seemed to become more obvious with each passing moment.

"Very high," muttered Mr Jones. He had an old, rasping voice which fitted with his dusty greying hair but not the quick movements of his hands or his alert eyes. "Two centres. One… close. The other… " he paused, and looked hard at Simon, "*very* close."

Mr Smith clapped his hands and stretched his mouth into another thin-lipped smile. "Well, well. Good job we came to investigate. A potentially dangerous leak, it would seem. We'll have to do some more tests. But just now – I wonder – could we perhaps…"

He moved towards Simon in a sudden rapid stride that took him halfway across the kitchen before either Simon or Cat could react. He was reaching out for Simon's shoulder, and Cat was just about to shout at him, when there was a phenomenal explosion of banging from the front door.

Mr Smith and Mr Jones froze. Mr Smith tipped his head to one side, as if listening intently, and then bared his teeth in an angry snarl.

"Jemmet," he said under his breath to Mr Jones, who flicked the briefcase shut in one smooth movement. The two stood and bowed slightly to Simon and Cat.

"Afraid we must be off," said Mr Smith. "But that's a nasty leak. We'll be back soon to seal it off for you. Good day."

The loud banging resumed. With an irritated glance at the hallway, the two of them sidled out through the back door into the garden, just as the front door crashed open. Almost immediately a short, fat, balding man in blue overalls burst into the kitchen. He looked rapidly round the room, strode to the back door, and peered out into the garden.

"Gone," he said, with great satisfaction, and then turned to the children with a wide smile.

"Albert Jemmet," he said, in a friendly voice. "Emergency Electrics Limited." He pointed at a badge on his blue overalls, which had a green lightning strike above the words *Electrical Disturbances and Emergency Repairs.* "I used to look after any little problems in the house for your great-aunt. Your mum was kind enough to keep me on when you moved in." He stuck out his hand. "At your service."

Cat gaped at him. She felt as if nothing that had happened that morning made any sense at all, least of all this jolly, balding man in blue overalls, but she shook his hand limply, and then sat down rather hard at the kitchen table.

"How… how did you get in?" she asked.

Albert Jemmet looked a little shifty.

"Ah, well, you left the door open," he said. "And since I was getting very high readings, I thought maybe I would just let myself in to check that everything was all right."

Cat frowned. She had definitely shut the door, she was sure of it. But on the other hand, Albert Jemmet was an altogether friendlier intruder than Mr Smith and Mr Jones, and he seemed to have scared them off, so maybe they should be grateful.

"Have they really gone?" said Simon, looking rather pale. "The other two?"

Cat got up and peered out of the kitchen window. All she could see was the bare, wintry garden, with its straggly lawn, overgrown pond, and rather forlorn-looking bare trees. There was no one in sight.

"They've gone," she said to Simon, who gave a great sigh of relief. He looked across at Albert Jemmet, who gave him a friendly grin.

"Well, young lady," Albert said, turning to Cat. "A cup of tea would be extremely nice, if you could spare the hot water."

Cat hesitated. Albert Jemmet was a complete stranger, even if he did say he'd known Great-Aunt Irene. Entertaining complete strangers at the kitchen table when Mum was away was not on the list of permitted activities.

"Could we see some proof of identity?" she said, politely.

"Of course," said Albert Jemmet, looking business-like, and he handed over a card and a number of leaflets. *Emergency Electrics Ltd* had a website, an email address, and a phone number, as well as a motto: *Solving your emergencies with emergency solutions*. Albert Jemmet was listed on his business card as Senior Emergency Call-out Operative.

"Actually," he said, tapping the card, "there's only me. But people like to feel you're part of a bigger organisation."

Cat raised her eyebrows at Simon. He nodded. Albert Jemmet seemed to be quite genuine.

"Well, then, a cup of tea," Cat said briskly. "How do you have it?"

"Milk, six sugars please," said Albert Jemmet, and patted his large stomach with a grin. "I've cut back. Used to be twelve."

As Cat made the tea, Albert Jemmet rummaged in an old canvas bag he had brought with him. Out of it came various odd mechanical devices, which he proceeded to tap, twiddle and peer at while pointing them in different directions around the room. Simon noticed that Albert seemed especially keen to point them down at the table, right in the direction of the sword on his knees, which he could feel tingling.

"My own inventions, mostly," he said, seeing Simon watching him. "Very delicate. Attuned to particular sorts of electrical energy."

He put a strange blue monocle in his right eye and took a quick glance at the table before turning his attention to the light bulb overhead.

"Ah… hmm," he said, and took the monocle out of his eye. Cat handed him a mug of tea, and he took a great slurp of it with evident enjoyment.

"Lovely," he said, with a sigh, and then looked seriously at Simon.

"Well then. Very clear case of electrical disturbance here. Displacing objects, attracting the likes of Smith and Jones. I'd say you're very lucky I happened to be in the neighbourhood."

"Who are they – those other two? Smith and Jones?" asked Simon. Albert looked grim.

"Rival outfit," he said. "I wouldn't have much to do with them if I were you. Nasty creatures. Best not to let them in at all."

"I didn't have any choice," said Cat indignantly. "They just pushed in. Rather… well… rather like *you*, Mr Jemmet."

Albert Jemmet grinned, and didn't seem in the least bit abashed.

"Call me Albert," he said. "No need to be formal." He nodded at them both cheerily, then drained his tea and pushed his chair back.

"Well, I must be getting on. But, before I go, I wonder if you've had any… odd things appearing in the house? Anything – well, anything that shouldn't be here. Doesn't belong. If I'm going to fix your little problem, I'd really need to see them… do a few more tests."

Simon looked up, his dark watchful eyes meeting Albert Jemmet's shrewd blue ones.

"No," he said. "There hasn't been anything."

There was a stillness in the kitchen, and then Albert shrugged, and laughed.

"Well, there we are, then. But I'll leave you my card, in case. You can contact me on my mobile – day or night… Especially night," he added, after a pause.

He gathered up his canvas bag and bustled out of the kitchen. "I'll let myself out," he called cheerily from the hall, and then the children heard the door slam shut.

Silence settled on the house. Cat felt stunned by the morning's events. She looked at Simon, one eyebrow raised, and he brought the sword out from under the table. He weighed it in his hands, and then put it down carefully in front of her.

"Do you think we should have shown it to him?" said Cat. "He said anything odd, that doesn't belong... Is the sword something to do with the radiation they were measuring? Do you think it's dangerous?"

Simon shook his head. "I don't know about radiation, but I'm pretty sure it's not dangerous. It doesn't *feel* dangerous anyway. It feels... friendly, somehow."

They both looked at the long, shining blade on the kitchen table, utterly real and yet utterly out of place. Cat felt a slight shiver down her spine. When she was younger, she had longed for magic to be real. She and Simon had played endless games of make-believe, trying to find hidden doors to another world, or pretending to turn themselves invisible. But however many times they'd rubbed crystals or shut themselves in wardrobes, they'd never succeeded in making anything the least bit out of the ordinary happen. And now, here was an ancient broadsword sitting in the middle of the table, apparently arrived from nowhere.

She shook her head, as if to clear water out of her ears. There was bound to be an ordinary explanation.

"It's Mum's, I bet," she said, firmly. "I must have just missed it when I came downstairs."

"Maybe…" said Simon, but he was certain the sword had nothing to do with Mum. It was odd, and out of place, and yet there was also something about it… something that Simon almost recognised.

As his fingers ran along the shining length of the sword, he suddenly noticed that the kitchen table was emptier than it should have been.

"Cat?" he said, annoyed. "Have you taken my DS?"

Chapter Three

Jem was not entirely happy about having to accompany Dora on the journey to the city. He had various bits of mischief planned for the Summer Fair, and the ongoing feud between the castle servant boys and the castle squires was reaching a critical stage. Without Jem, the plan to steal all the squires' undergarments and hang them on a line over the battlements was not going to happen. But on the other hand, he would be going to the palace. None of the other servant boys had even been to the city, never mind visited Queen Igraine's court, so Jem was looking forward to lording it over everyone when he returned. Even better, it seemed they were going to take the short cut, straight through the Great Forest, and that meant he might even get to meet one of the mysterious forest folk who were said to live there. The only drawback, as far as Jem could see, was having to make the trip with the unutterably wet apprentice witch, Dora.

Dora herself felt pretty much the same way about having to have Jem along. When she'd first arrived at Roland Castle, six months ago, she had found everything utterly overwhelming. She was never quite sure what to say, or how to behave – who was important and who wasn't. But out of everyone at the castle, Jem had probably been the hardest to work out – and the most annoying. He was supposed to be a kitchen boy, but he had spent most of his time since he could walk hanging about in the stables, or practising archery, or sword fighting. When he wasn't stealing food, fighting, or leading the other servant boys in an all-out battle with the squires, he was out hunting with someone else's hawk.

No one seemed to be able to control him, except occasionally Sir Mortimer Roland, the lord of the castle. Nobody knew who Jem's father had been, and his mother had given up trying to discipline him at the age of four, when he had flooded the whole castle by stuffing three fat hens down the main drain. And then just a few months ago he'd set the east wing of the castle on fire after hatching six red dragons down in the stables. A couple of the baby dragons were still hanging around the castle, convinced Jem was their mother.

"Why Jem?" she complained to Lizzie while she packed her bags. "Of all the people the Druid could have chosen! He's bound to get us into trouble, or upset someone important, and we'll be marched back to the castle in disgrace."

"I'm sure it will be fine," said Lizzie, soothingly. "He's fourteen, and very good with a sword, and he's clever. You won't get tricked out of your money or robbed with Jem there. Plus he knows all the roads between here and the forest. He spent all last summer helping Old Tom take the goats to market."

"Until that time he smuggled one of them into Lady Alys's chambers and it ate all her dresses," Dora pointed out. She sighed. That was exactly the sort of trick Jem was famous for, and exactly why she didn't want him along. He'd spend the whole time playing tricks on her, she just knew it.

Dora gathered up her travelling bags reluctantly,

gave Lizzie a hug, and went to meet Jem at the castle gates. He was swaggering around, whistling loudly and looking like he'd been waiting all day. Sol the butcher's boy was there with him, along with Violet and her bunch of girly friends, making eyes at Jem and giggling at everything he said.

Dora put on her blankest expression as she walked towards the group. But luckily, just as she got there, Sir Mortimer arrived and ordered all the onlookers to get on with their duties.

"The Druid's been called away," he said. "Fire at the mill. He asked me to see you both off and make sure you had everything you needed."

Dora's heart sank. The Druid had already shown her the magic she needed to get into the forest, but she'd still been hoping to see him for some last-minute advice and encouragement before she left. Besides, Sir Mortimer was the lord of the castle, and always made her feel horribly nervous.

"It's the queen's nephew, Lord Ravenglass, you need to take the objects to," Sir Mortimer said, looking sternly at them both. "He pretty much runs things now, I've heard. You'll need this letter of introduction." He tucked a piece of parchment inside Jem's pack. "Keep it safe, they won't let you in without it! And here's five silver coins – Dora, best to trust you with these, I think – should see you there and back. Have you got the goggling glasses safe? And the picture box?"

Dora nodded, and patted her pack.

Jem coughed, importantly.

"There's a new one, too," he said, looking pleased with himself. "*I* found it this morning."

He held up a smooth, shiny object, a little bit like the camera but flatter, and a bright red colour, like the ripest strawberries. Then, with a flourish, he opened it out. It opened like a book, but one with thick covers and no pages. Inside was another small window like the camera, and a number of strange buttons.

"Another one?" said Sir Mortimer, looking troubled. "And you found it this morning? The Druid ought to see this…"

"Yes," said Jem. "Or we could just take it along with the others? I mean, we're only supposed to take them to the palace. We don't need to know what they are."

It was true, they didn't, but Dora felt a little uneasy. She tried to think what the Druid had said, about the other worlds. She had a feeling that if two objects from the same place was odd, three must be even more so.

Sir Mortimer hesitated, but then shrugged, and clapped them both on the back. "Well, there's nothing for it. There's a cart to Bridbury waiting outside to give you a lift, and if you don't leave now, you won't get to the Great Forest before dark."

He shepherded them outside the castle gates and towards the cart, which was full of noisy sheep being transported to market, then raised his hand in farewell.

"Off you go. Travel safely, be careful, and don't show *anyone* you meet those peculiar… whatever-they-ares. Good luck!"

As they rattled off, Dora heard a loud squeal and looked up to see Violet leaning dangerously far out over the battlements and waving her handkerchief.

"Goodbye, darlingest Jem!" she trilled. "Bring me back a present from the city! And try to be nice to Dora for me – she can't *help* being so clumsy and boring!"

Dora went red and stared at her feet, wishing

she could just turn Violet into a toad, right now. But she was so busy concentrating on *not* doing a spell, that she didn't notice Jem's raised eyebrows, or see him making a very rude gesture at Violet.

The first part of the journey was uneventful, if not exactly comfortable. Travelling in a rickety cart with twenty noisy sheep was like being stuck in the middle of a panicked crowd all shouting at once. At least, Dora thought, all the bleating meant she didn't have to talk to Jem, even if it was quite annoying having wet sheep noses pushed down her back, and having her hair constantly nibbled.

Jem, she noticed, was absorbed in the strange red book. He was bent over it in fierce concentration, fiddling endlessly with the buttons and impatiently flicking away his red hair as it fell into his eyes. He barely seemed to notice the sheep. He simply elbowed them out of the way whenever they stuck their curious sheep faces in between him and the book.

Dora watched him crossly. Not only was he an annoying, swaggering know-it-all, he also seemed to think he was in charge of the third strange object, just because he had found it. *And* it looked like he was now firmly part of Violet's nasty little gang. She decided that she would try and have as little to do with him as possible on the journey, and she was definitely not going to give him any chance to be 'nice' to her.

They got to Bridbury, a small market town on the edge of the forest, just before dark. In the bustle of finding a place to stay and organising food, there was little time for conversation. Dora began to hope that if she simply rolled herself up in her blanket and pretended she was asleep, she might be able to get through the first day without exchanging more than a dozen words in total. But she'd reckoned without Jem. He was dying to show off his discoveries about the shiny new object.

"It's a magic fortune-telling book," he announced with a flourish as soon as the door to their room was shut. "I've worked out how to use it – look!"

He opened the book, and pressed a few buttons. The dark window lit up with stars and moving patterns which slowly became a picture of a castle with strange symbols scattered across it.

Jem's fingers flew over the buttons once more, and a number of recognisable characters started to flick across the screen.

"There!" said Jem, triumphantly, as the pictures stopped moving. A small, fierce-looking knight was standing in front of them, waving his sword.

"It's Sir Roderick," said Jem, and Dora had to agree, it looked very like him.

"Now watch," said Jem, and pressed a few more buttons. The figure marched up and down and round a few corners. Stars appeared, then gold coins. After a frenzied minute or two more of Jem's fingers and thumbs dancing over the buttons, the picture froze again and Sir Mortimer stood next to an enormous pile of gold.

"You see?" said Jem proudly. "It's a fortune-telling book. Sir Roderick is going to get a pile of gold. He's obviously going to win the Autumn Joust."

Dora looked at the peculiar object, frowning. Something didn't seem quite right about this explanation. If the shiny book was from another world, like the other objects seemed to be, how could it tell them anything real about *their* world? But on the other hand, the figure did look rather like Sir Roderick, and it *was* quite likely that he would win the Autumn Joust.

Curious, she moved closer, forgetting her vow to have as little to do with Jem as possible. She peered over Jem's shoulders at the pictures in the dark window.

"Does it show anyone else's fortune?" she asked.

Jem's fingers flickered across the buttons, and a new set of characters paraded across the little window. He stopped at an image of a stocky boy with a shock of red hair.

"That's me," he said. "I found myself earlier. Now – watch this!"

The boy on the screen set off at a pace, with strange objects whizzing past him in a way that made Dora feel quite dizzy. When the picture finally stopped moving, the boy was flat on his back with stars floating above his head, and a fat knight with an axe was standing over him grinning.

Dora couldn't help giggling. Jem frowned.

"That didn't happen last time. Last time I got a pile of gold, just like Sir Mortimer. Rats! What's wrong with the stupid thing?"

"Maybe you're going to get a pile of gold, and then a fat knight is going to whack you over the head and steal it?" suggested Dora, with a bubble of laughter in her voice.

Jem snorted, and fiddled again, till he'd got a picture of a girl with dark hair in what looked very like the dress of an apprentice witch.

"Let's see what's in store for you, then," he said. Dora watched the girl whizzing over the picture and held her breath. She was pretty sure the red book couldn't tell the future, but she still felt quite anxious that her small copy didn't end up knocked out by a fat knight.

When the picture finally settled, Dora couldn't help clapping her hands. The small witch was now dressed in shining gold and had a crown of flowers.

"I'm going to be queen of the May!" she whooped, and completely forgetting herself, punched Jem on the arm in delight. He raised one eyebrow, and she immediately felt covered in confusion. She looked at her feet.

"Is that what you want to be – queen of the May?" he said scornfully.

"Well, it's better than being hit on the head

by a fat knight," said Dora, looking up crossly. "Why? What do *you* want? A pile of gold?"

Jem looked at her, as if deciding whether to bother to reply. After a moment, he threw himself down on the nearby bed with a sigh, and stared up at the ceiling with his hands behind his head.

"I want adventures," he said, with a faraway look in his eyes. "I'm a commoner so I'm not allowed to be a knight. But all the squires are a bunch of stuck-up idiots who can't see past the end of their own noses. I'd make a much better knight than any of them. I want to travel the world, see dragons in the mountains, find treasure, rescue damsels. One day, I'm going to. You wait and see."

And with that, he wrapped himself in his blanket and turned on his side, facing the wall. Dora slipped quietly into bed on the opposite side of the room, but they both lay awake for a while. Dora was thinking about Jem, and wondering whether he'd make a good knight if he ever had the chance. She decided he'd probably be terrible – he was far too disobedient.

Jem was thinking about the strange book, and Dora. She was like a mouse most of the time, he thought, and quite prickly and unfriendly. But then just for a moment she had seemed like she might be quite fun, before she got all prickly again.

Jem shoved the box under his pillow. He felt a shiver of excitement at the thought that tomorrow they would be entering the Great Forest. He wondered if the fortune-telling box had any of the forest folk in it.

Chapter Four

Simon and Cat had argued all day over what to tell their mum about the sword. Simon had wanted to keep it secret. There was something about the strange, intricate engravings along the blade and the smooth, worn feel of the hilt that was familiar. It felt as if it had always belonged to him, and he didn't want anyone taking it away. But Cat still half thought it might be Mum's from work, and they would definitely have some explaining to do if it *was* hers and she found they'd hidden it.

In the end, they decided to just show it to her, and if it was clear it wasn't hers, they could say Simon had found it in the cellar. There was plenty of old junk down there, and it was all Great-Aunt Irene's, so there'd be no need for Mum to fuss about who the sword belonged to if they'd found it there.

Florence Arnold got back from her conference late that evening, after being stuck in a traffic jam for hours, and required two cups of tea and a large slice of fruit cake before she had recovered enough to ask Simon and Cat how their day had been.

"Good," said Cat. "But we had some weird people knock on the door saying there was a radiation leak or something in the area – and then someone called Albert Jemmet came round – he said you knew him?"

Florence nodded, a little distractedly. "Yes, he was your great-aunt's odd-job man. He seemed very nice when I met him, I said we'd let him know if we needed anything. Did he say there was anything wrong?"

"Umm, something about electricity, I think," said Cat. "But it seems all right now. And then… Simon found this. Do you know what it is?"

As Simon brought the sword out and put it on the table, Florence was just picking up her third cup of tea. When she turned round and saw the shining blade in front of her, she went white and dropped the cup on the floor. The she sat down rather suddenly at the table and put her hand out to touch the sword, as if not quite sure it was real.

"Where did you find this?" she said.

Simon looked at Cat triumphantly. "In the cellar, behind some old boxes," he said.

"It's not yours, then, Mum?" Cat asked, as she picked up the dropped cup and mopped up the tea from the floor.

Florence shook her head, and pulled the sword towards her. She looked carefully at the engraved symbols, tracing the shapes with her fingers.

"Where do you think it came from?" said Simon after a few minutes.

She looked up at him with an odd expression, wary and a little sad, and took a deep breath.

"It was your dad's," she said. "It's your dad's sword."

Simon and Cat looked at each other. Simon felt a strange mix of queasiness and excitement inside, as if he'd just swooped down a roller coaster ride. He wondered if that was why the sword had felt so special, so familiar somehow. Had he seen it before, when he was very little? Had he seen his dad using it?

"I didn't know Dad had a sword!" said Cat, passing Florence another tea then sitting down at the table. She put her hand on the hilt and felt a trickle of sadness, thinking about her dad. "It's – isn't it old? It looks really old. And it feels weird."

Florence nodded, and turned the sword over, showing them some of the markings.

"It's very unusual. I'd know it anywhere. It's how we met, actually. He turned up at an exhibition I was helping organise, on ancient weaponry. Paul Rogers was there, giving a talk on Saxon fighting techniques, and your dad stood up and told him he was talking a load of old rubbish, and no one fought like that with a broadsword. Then he got his own out of a big old rucksack and started waving it around to show him. Cleared the lecture hall in about three seconds – everyone thought he was mad…!"

She laughed at the memory, and then dabbed her eyes with the edge of her cardigan.

"Oh dear. It was all such a long time ago.

The sword's not an original – you can see that there's no pitting or anything, so it's not that old. But it's not exactly a replica either. It's been made using the same kind of techniques as the Saxons used – fantastic craftsmanship. I never could get him to tell me where he got it, but he certainly knew how to use it."

She took a sip of tea, thoughtfully, her mind clearly in the past.

Simon started thinking about his dad. He couldn't really remember him, just vague fuzzy memories, like being lifted up in the air, or the feel of a bristly face against his cheek. He knew he'd been a historian, but not the sort who spent his life locked up in library archives. Gwyn Arnold had been more interested in the practical side of life in the Dark Ages. He taught people how to use ancient hunting techniques, how to survive in a wild forest, how to make a fire, or shelters, or build castle defences. Until one day he'd died in a car crash, and since then there had just been Simon and Cat, and their mum.

Simon didn't really remember his dad's death, and even Cat, who was five at the time, only vaguely remembered the funeral. He wondered sometimes what life would be like if their dad was still around, but mostly he was just used to the way things were.

"It's funny…" Florence said, cradling her cup

of tea and looking at the sword with a faraway expression in her eyes. "All this time it was here in this house – and I thought he'd given it to Lou."

"Uncle Lou?" said Cat, looking suddenly excited. "I remember Uncle Lou! But we haven't seen him for years! What happened to him?"

"Who's Uncle Lou?" Simon asked, although the name was vaguely familiar and comforting, like finding an old teddy bear you'd forgotten you once had.

Florence looked momentarily horrified and put her hand to her mouth, as if to cram the name back in, but it was too late. Both her children were looking up at her expectantly, memories of the tall, lanky, dark-haired man who'd been such a constant presence in their childhood suddenly crowding into their heads... She sighed.

"Lou was Great-Aunt Irene's son. Your father's cousin," said Florence, reluctantly. "He was around quite a bit when you were younger, but it's been a long time..."

"Aren't there some photos of him in the old album?" said Cat suddenly. "You know, the blue one – where is it? We haven't had it out for years!"

"It's in that grey box in my room," said Florence,

and then added, as if making the best of it, "Why don't you go and get it and we can have a look through the pictures."

When Cat came back down with the tatty blue photo album, Florence turned to the early photos, showing Simon as a baby, with his dad holding him up proudly, and two-year-old Cat looking utterly uninterested in the new arrival.

"There," said his mum, pointing her finger at a shadowy figure standing behind his dad. "That's Lou. He never did like being photographed, I only got that one because he wasn't paying attention."

Uncle Lou looked a little like a scarecrow, Simon thought – all long arms and legs and a shock of messy dark hair, looking slightly away from the camera, and half hidden by his dad. His dad was a much stockier figure, with strong arms and very fair curly hair, and a wide smile. Cat had inherited their dad's bright hair and blue eyes, he thought. His own was dark and straight, like Mum's. Like Uncle Lou's.

"He and your dad were cousins, but they seemed more like brothers," said Mum, smiling at the photo. "Irene took your dad in after his parents died, so they more or less grew up together.

Lou was a total computer geek, used to write games. Actually, that old game you like playing on your DS, Simon, the one with all the knights – that was one of his, originally."

"*Castle Quest?*" said Simon, surprised. "He *wrote* it?"

"Well, he wrote the prototype. He'd gone off travelling by the time it was made. But it was mostly his characters and his ideas."

"It's funny," said Cat, frowning. "I remember Uncle Lou now, but I'd hardly thought of him till you said his name."

She turned a few pages of the album, past the point where their father suddenly faded out of the family snaps, to one of her standing proudly in her new school uniform next to a pair of very long legs. "Look – there's one here – isn't that Uncle Lou?"

Florence nodded, and turned the page to another photo of Simon and Cat side by side on a bench, eating ice-cream.

"Look, that's when we went to Wareham!" she said brightly.

"I remember," said Simon, turning the page back. "I remember him taking *me* to school when

I first started, too. I don't know why I'd forgotten. But where did he go? And if he was Great-Aunt Irene's son, how come she left *us* the house, and not him?"

Florence sighed. "Well, she always said the house was meant to go to your dad, so after he died she said we should have it. There was some heirloom or other for Lou. But I don't know if she managed to pass it on to him – he disappeared years ago and he didn't come back for the funeral. I'm not sure she really knew how to get hold of him, they hadn't spoken in ages."

"So what happened to him?" said Cat, curious. "Why did he disappear?"

Florence's expression suddenly turned rather vague. "We had a bit of a row," she said. "When Simon was about five. He went off in a temper, decided he was going to travel the world."

"A row?" said Cat. "What about?"

"Nothing you need to worry about," said Florence briskly. She stood up. "Right, it's late. You need to get to bed, and so do I. The sword can go back down in the cellar, since it's been there safely all this time. Come on – upstairs. No arguments."

Simon knew better than to object, but he caught Cat's eye, and she nodded slightly. Much later, when Florence had turned off her light, Cat came padding up to Simon's attic room in her dressing-gown and slippers, and settled down on the end of his bed.

"We need to talk," she said. "Something odd's going on."

"I know," said Simon. "Mum was being weird. How can this sword be *Dad's*? And how come we'd completely forgotten Uncle Lou?"

Cat wrinkled up her nose, thinking hard.

"No idea. I suppose it's possible I just got used to him not being there and forgot about him, but – I don't know – that seems unlikely. I must have been *seven* when he went. He practically lived with us most of the time we were little. And then… he just didn't come round any more." She frowned. "And then there's the sword. Mum didn't leave it there, you were right."

"Do you think Uncle Lou had anything to do with it?" said Simon.

"What, like he sneaked in and left it on the stairs?" said Cat doubtfully.

They looked at each other. It wasn't a very

comforting idea, that someone could have broken into the house in the early morning and left a whacking great sword on the stairs. But otherwise, the sword had just appeared on its own, and that wasn't a very comforting idea either.

"Could he have anything to do with those people in suits?" said Simon. "The radiation people – Smith and Jones. Could one of those have been…?"

"Uncle Lou?" said Cat, sounding shocked. "No way! They were creepy. He was never, ever, creepy! He was always joking and being an idiot. He was more like the other one. Albert Jemmet. But tall and thin." She chewed her thumbnail, deep in thought. "The sword," she said, tentatively. "How come it *felt* so strange?"

Simon was quiet for a moment, then he got out of bed and went across to his chest of drawers. He rummaged in his sock drawer, and then came back holding out a small wooden box.

"I thought it felt a bit like this," he said, and held out the object to Cat. "I was going to show you once I'd got it open, but – well, maybe you'd better have a look now."

It was a narrow jewellery box of dark wood,

with strange markings on the top. There were three deeply carved symbols, and just above them, a carving of what looked like a precious stone. It had been painted, once, but the paint was faded, and almost worn off. It was just possible to see that the stone had been coloured a deep orange-yellow, like a fiery sunset.

Cat took the box, and almost dropped it.

"You're right!" she said. "It's just like the sword, all prickly and electric." She looked accusingly at Simon. "Where did it come from? When did you find it? Why didn't you *tell* me?"

"I found it under the floor just by my bed, a few days ago," he said. "A bit of Lego went down a crack between the floorboards, and I was digging around trying to get hold of it when I realised one of the boards was loose. So I pulled it up to see if I could find the Lego piece, and the box was just there. I *was* going to tell you – I just wanted to see if I could open it first."

Cat tried to lift the lid of the box, getting her fingernails under and pulling from different sides. But although there didn't seem to be a lock of any sort, the box remained firmly closed.

Simon shook his head. "It's no good – I've tried

everything. I even tried to get my penknife in and prise it open." He rummaged in his drawer again and brought out his Swiss Army Knife to show her – the end of the blade had been snapped off cleanly.

Cat frowned at the box, and then ran her fingers over the symbols on the top.

"There's something about these," she said. "They look familiar. I'm sure I've seen them somewhere before… Maybe they're a clue about how to open it."

"Should we show it to Mum, do you think?" said Simon. He looked at her with a very neutral expression.

Cat met his gaze. "We should, you know," she said. "After all, it must have belonged to Great-Aunt Irene. So it's Mum's, really."

There was a moment's silence.

Then Cat raised one eyebrow. "But… she did say we could have anything we wanted from Great-Aunt Irene's things. And neither of us has chosen anything yet. So…"

"… we could choose this," finished Simon.

They grinned at each other, then Cat dug in her dressing-gown pocket and pulled out the card

Albert Jemmet had left. She twirled it in between her fingers.

"You know, I really didn't want to move here," she said. "I thought it would be boring. But right now I'm beginning to think it might have... *interesting* possibilities."

Chapter Five

The Great Forest was old, and peculiar. It had always been part of the kingdom, but the forest had its own laws, and you couldn't enter it without magic. Very few people had ever met any of the folk who lived there, and those who had couldn't agree on what they looked like. Some said they were tall and thin, with faintly green skin, while others swore they were short, fat men with long beards who smelled of the earth. The innkeeper who'd pointed out the way to Dora and Jem said the only forest folk he'd ever seen had been three inches high, with wings.

It had taken them about an hour to reach the edge of the forest from Bridbury. Now the outer trees loomed above them, large and forbidding, and the way forward appeared to be barred by a tapestry of dark thorny brambles and vines growing between the trunks.

"Now what?" said Jem, dumping his pack on the ground. "We can't get through there. What a waste of time. We've obviously gone the wrong way."

Dora slipped her own pack off her shoulder and flexed her fingers. "You have to use a finding spell to see the path," she told him. "The Druid showed me."

"Oh, of course!" said Jem, his face clearing. "That'll be why I had to have you along, instead of just going by myself. To do the magic. Well, come on then, Dora, get on with it."

He grinned at her, and Dora wondered if he knew how annoying he was being. She suspected he did, and that just made her feel even more cross. Trust Jem to think that he was the messenger and she was just along to help him, when it was completely the other way round. And he might need her, for her magic, but she wasn't sure exactly what she needed *him* for.

Dora turned to face the forest, a scowl on her face. She held out her hands and said the exact words of the spell the Druid had shown her.

Almost immediately, a path appeared in the gap – it was narrow, and slightly ghostly, a pale ribbon slipping in between the gnarled trunks and on into the cool shadows. Jem hesitated, looked at Dora with one eyebrow raised, then shouldered his pack and strode forward with a cheerful whistle.

Dora trudged after him, seething. There he was, swaggering his way through the Great Forest whistling, when everyone knew that you had to be extremely respectful and *extremely* humble in the Great Forest. Expecting Jem to be humble was like expecting a hawk to roost with the chickens.

Suddenly Jem stopped, and held up his hand.

"Can you hear something?" he whispered.

Dora looked behind her. She could no longer see the place where they had entered. Branches swept low across the path, and the gleam of sunlight from beyond the edge of the trees was barely visible. Everything was still, and quiet. Then, just as she was about to shake her head, she heard a faint hiss, coming from up ahead. She froze. The hiss was followed by a clanking sound, and then what sounded like a whistle.

Jem's hand went to his short sword. He eased

it out of the scabbard, and gestured to her to get behind him. "Follow me – stay close," he mouthed, and set off cautiously up the path.

Dora stayed about as close as she could without tripping him up, her ears straining for the faint metallic clanking up ahead. As they moved forward, the sounds got louder, and they could see wisps of smoke filtering through the trees. Suddenly, there was a huge shriek, and a sound like thunder. The ground under their feet shook, and a shadow seemed to pass through the trees to their left.

Dora and Jem froze.

But then slowly the noise and tremors faded, moving off deeper into the forest, away from the path.

Jem shrugged, and put his sword away.

"It's gone. Probably just the forest folk," he said, and clapped her on the shoulder. "No need to be scared, Dora. There's bound to be a few odd noises in a place like this."

But before Dora could answer, he had set off up the path again, whistling tunefully. Dora gritted her teeth, and headed after him.

It was about mid morning when they reached a fork in the path. They were now deep in the forest, and their footsteps were barely leaving any mark in the soft layers of dead leaves. Jem's whistling had finally died away under the weight of the surrounding silence. The light had faded to a greenish dimness, and when Jem turned round, Dora could only just see his pale face in front of her.

"So... which way, do you think?" said Jem, pointing to the fork. To their right, the path broadened and became flatter and straighter. To the left, it wound further into the trees, like a narrow dark river.

"I don't know," said Dora. "There's only supposed to be one way – and the Druid said we mustn't stray off it."

"I think we need to take the left-hand fork," said Jem. "I think that's the real path."

"Are you sure?" said Dora, taken aback. "The other one looks much better used."

Jem gave her a superior look.

"That's what you're meant to think. It's an illusion, obviously. To catch out the unwary traveller. We'll take the left-hand path, because we're not idiots."

Dora frowned. She really didn't like the look of the left-hand path, but Jem was already heading firmly up it — and there was a certain sense to what he'd said. Everyone knew the forest was tricky, so things were not likely to be what they seemed. Perhaps Jem was right, and the obvious-looking path was the false one. She shrugged, and followed him.

It wasn't long before Dora was regretting her decision, and wishing she'd never even *heard* of Jem, never mind had to travel halfway across the kingdom with him. She was pretty sure they were lost. And ever since they'd moved onto the narrow dark path the forest had been getting stranger and stranger. There were noises, now, from all directions — weird screeches and howls and the grinding of metal on metal. Sometimes Dora thought she could see a movement — a shadow, a gleam of silver, a flash of some bright colour — but then it was gone, and all they could see around them were trees.

She and Jem were sticking very closely together, and Jem had his hand permanently on his sword. Suddenly, without warning, there was a booming sound and the light in the forest became incredibly bright. Dora could feel hot sun on the back of her neck, and her feet appeared to be crunching across yellow sand. She clutched Jem, both of them dazzled momentarily by the reflections of sunlight on water. There appeared to be people not far away, and Dora could see rocks. Great blue waves were crashing down on the rocks and sending up plumes of spray.

But before Dora and Jem had a chance to move, or say anything, the dim greenness of the forest closed in around them again, and there was just soft leaf-mould under their feet, and no sound but the branches rustling gently in a faint breeze. Where the sea had been crashing down on the rocks, there a little bit to her right, there appeared to be nothing but mossy green undergrowth and trailing brambles.

Jem looked at Dora, and she looked back, wide-eyed. Neither of them quite dared to say a word. But the forest continued to stretch out silently around them with no apparent changes, and suddenly Dora realised she was still clutching Jem's arm. She let go hurriedly, and moved away.

Jem straightened up, and took his hand off his

sword hilt. "Shall we… er… carry on?" he said, in a slightly shaky voice.

Dora nodded. She didn't trust herself to speak.

And then they both heard a rasping, snorting sound that was very, very close indeed.

They froze.

The snorting got louder, and suddenly they could see the shadow of a huge creature moving between the trees, right next to where they were frozen to the spot. Jem started to ease his short sword out of its scabbard again, and they both started to slowly back away down the path.

Dora could see flashes of grey between the trees, and hear the crack of branches snapping. Whatever it was, it was enormous, and it wasn't disappearing. In fact, it seemed to be getting closer, and Dora was pretty sure Jem's sword was not going to be of any use at all. Her legs were feeling like they didn't quite belong to her, and she rapidly started reviewing the possible spells she could use.

At that moment an immense wall of grey flesh came crashing out of a clump of trees ahead of them, and Dora screamed. The creature was like nothing she'd ever seen before. It was the size of the castle gatehouse, and it had four massive thick grey legs and huge flapping ears. Some kind of grey arm was waving angrily from the front of its face, while two huge white fangs curved out of the front of its mouth. It was screeching like a hundred horses neighing all at once, and they could hear the sound of trees splintering and cracking as the creature hurled itself towards them.

"Run!" shouted Jem. "I'll try and hold it off!"

Dora watched in horror as Jem threw himself in front of her, waving his sword and shouting. The creature hesitated for a moment, as if confused, and then lowered its head and charged at the tiny figure.

Dora raised her hands. She gabbled the words of a shrinking spell, threw all the magic she could muster at the huge grey beast, and shut her eyes tight.

There was a sudden silence. When Dora opened her eyes, the creature seemed to have disappeared. But unfortunately, so had Jem.

Chapter Six

Simon woke suddenly, with a sense that something was very wrong. His room was silent, and dark, but he had a feeling that he had been woken by the crash of something falling. The silence around him seemed to shiver with the aftershock... He held his breath and lay still, trying to work out what had happened. He had been dreaming of a mountainous land, with sheer cliffs plummeting to deep stony rivers, and there had been reddish creatures with leathery bat wings, swirling in the sky above him...

Simon jumped, startled. A small, rasping sound was coming from the direction of his wardrobe. He heard it again - it was like something being rubbed along the edge of the wooden door. There was a small flutter, like air whispering through the central heating pipes, then a distinct chirrup.

He reached out one arm and switched on the bedside lamp. As the room flicked into sight, he found himself staring into the intelligent black eye of what looked like a small red pterodactyl, perched on the end of his bed. It cocked its head and stretched out its wings for a second, and as it did so a second identical creature squawked from the top of the wardrobe.

Simon felt as if a cold finger was tracing a line down his spine. The creatures in his room couldn't be real – yet he could smell a faint burning smell coming from them, feel the air move as they beat their wings, hear their rasping croaks. They looked exactly like the creatures from his dream. But how could they be here, in his room? They didn't even *exist*.

They bobbed their heads and shuffled from foot to foot, and then the one on the wardrobe decided to fly down. It crashed into his overhead light, sending it swinging wildly, while the creature ricocheted off and flapped desperately as it slid down the wall to his armchair. Then the other one took off and flew straight into the glass of his window, scrabbling uselessly at it for a few seconds before wheeling around for another attempt.

Simon, protecting his head as best he could with his arms, tried to open the window before the creature dive-bombed him. It was like the time a pigeon had got into the living room by mistake, but this was worse, because there were two of them, and they were the size of large seagulls. The first one kept throwing itself at the window, while the other was squawking and trying to disentangle itself from the heap of clothes strewn over Simon's chair.

Finally, he wrenched the window open, and the first creature flew out with a screech like a hunting owl. It wasn't long before the other had followed it – both of them, Simon thought, were clearly considerably more intelligent than pigeons. He wasn't quite sure whether that was a good or bad thing.

He banged the window shut hurriedly, and sat down on the edge of his bed, breathing hard. The room seemed undamaged, and miraculously, no one seemed to have heard the commotion. Simon looked at his alarm clock. One in the morning. Urgh. And he had school tomorrow.

As he sat there in the deepening silence, the whole episode began to seem unreal. Had there actually been pterodactyls in his bedroom? Had he just dreamed the whole thing?

He shivered, crawled back under his comforting duvet, and turned off the lamp. He'd worry about it in the morning.

"Simon! *Simon!*"

The voice was low and urgent, and insistent. Simon tried to unglue his eyes, but it felt like he was a hundred metres under water and was only slowly swimming up to the surface.

"Simon! Wake *up!*"

It was Cat, and she was shaking him, her voice hissing in his ear. He opened his eyes, and saw that it was morning. His sister was kneeling by the side of his bed, looking worried, and suddenly he remembered the creatures from his dream. Had they been real after all? Had they somehow got back in the house?

"Wh– wha?" he asked, a bit gummily, as he raised his head. "Wha'sit?"

Cat put her finger to her lips with a warning look, then leaned closer and spoke in a low voice.

"There's someone downstairs. Mum left for work ages ago, but I heard something downstairs, and when I leant over the banisters, I saw someone in a black suit going into the kitchen."

Simon immediately felt very wide awake.

"A black suit? Like…"

"Yes," said Cat. "It was one of the radiation people, I'm sure it was. They have a funny way of walking. I think it was the older one. Jones. But I can hear voices, so they must both be down there."

Simon sat up and pulled the duvet round his knees. He looked quickly around the room for the wooden box, and then saw it, sitting safely on his bedside table.

"Where's the sword?" he said.

"I don't know," said Cat. "I think Mum put it down in the cellar, after we went to bed. But they've got that machine, haven't they? They'll be able to trace it… or anything else strange in the house."

She looked at the box, and Simon reached out and slipped it under his pillow.

They could both hear the noises from downstairs now. There was a crash that sounded like a kitchen chair falling over, and then the bang of the back door – or was it the cellar door? There was silence for a minute, then the stomp of footsteps along the hall, followed by what sounded like someone knocking over the hat stand and cursing in a loud voice.

They looked at each other in sudden relief.

"That wasn't Smith or Jones!"

"That was— "

"Albert Jemmet!"

Nervously, in case Smith or Jones was still there, they crept out of Simon's bedroom and peered down the stairs. It was indeed Albert Jemmet, just picking himself up off the floor and replacing the tall wooden hat stand in the corner of the hallway.

"Mr Jemmet!" called Simon, and a jolly face looked up at them, smiling cheerily.

"Good morning!" he said. "Nothing to worry about – just me down here now. What do you say to a spot of breakfast?"

Simon padded into the kitchen after Cat to find Albert cracking eggs into a large frying pan and slicing bread for the toaster. Next to him stood a strange contraption. It was rather like an old-fashioned bicycle horn attached to a paint spray can. Simon could see a black rubber bulb and a trumpet-like mouthpiece, and under them both a small brass cannister.

"My fumigator," said Albert, picking it up and squeezing the bulb. A fine mist sprayed from the mouthpiece towards Simon and he caught a fresh smell of new-mown grass, overlaid with a faint tang of wood smoke. Then it was gone, and all he could smell was frying eggs.

"I got a call from… your mum. Asking me to come over and check your pest problem," said Albert, gesturing with the fumigator. "And while I was here, I thought I'd dish you up some breakfast and we'd have a little chat."

"Pest problem? What pest problem?" said Cat. "And I thought you were electricals anyway."

"Ah, yes," said Albert, sliding two fried eggs onto buttered toast and plonking it down on the table. "Well, pests are one of my sidelines."

He handed them each a card, a green one this time, with *Albert Jemmet, Senior Pest Control Executive* embossed on one side. On the other side was a black rat in silhouette and the words

All your pests dealt with, no questions asked.

"But we don't have any pests," said Cat. "Did Mum really ask you to come? And what about… I thought I saw…?"

She trailed off as Albert lifted up his fumigator and directed it with a stern expression at a large black feather lying close to the back door. It looked like a crow's feather, thought Simon, but what was any sort of feather doing in the kitchen? As the fumigator's spray reached it, the feather suddenly curled up and dissolved in a fine scattering of grey ash.

Albert looked pleased with himself and put his contraption back on the kitchen table.

"*No questions asked,*" he said meaningfully, and tapped the side of his nose with his finger. "Although," he continued cheerfully, "in this case, that's not strictly true. I *do* need to ask a few questions, as it happens. So – tuck into your eggs, and then we'll have a little talk, shall we?"

Simon and Cat looked at each other, and then sat down at the table. Ever since he had found the sword, Simon felt as if the world around him had shifted. It felt as if he suddenly had extra senses he'd never needed to use before.

Albert Jemmet seemed to have some connection to all this weirdness, and Simon wanted to hear what he had to say.

There was a pause, while Albert got stuck into his own eggs. In what seemed like a very short time he had polished them off and wiped the last piece of toast round his plate. He sat back, produced a wooden toothpick from his overall pocket, and started to chew the end absently.

"So," he said at last. "Let's get a grip on what's been happening here. How many things have gone missing, exactly?"

"Missing?" said Cat.

"Yes. Lost, disappeared, can't put your hand to them, sure you left them just there in plain sight but they've gone. You know – annoying stuff. How many?"

Simon and Cat exchanged glances.

"Your camera," Simon said triumphantly. "I *told* you it wasn't my fault."

Albert guffawed. "Well now. That depends. Not *entirely* your fault, I think we can agree. Anything else?"

"Yes,' said Simon. "My DS. Yesterday. I'm sure I left it on the kitchen table."

"Nothing else?" said Albert.

"I don't think so," said Cat. "Not that we've noticed."

"So," said Albert, tapping his teeth absently with the toothpick. "A couple of things from your side, plus maybe one or two other small bits you haven't noticed… Then there's the two baby red dragons I've had to send home this morning. Found them hanging around your garden."

"Baby *dragons*?" said Cat, not quite sure she'd heard right.

Simon gulped. So the creatures in his room *were* real after all. They were dragons!

"Yes," said Albert. "Caused me no end of trouble trying to catch them. Claws like knives. But I know there's at least one other thing that's appeared in this house that's not meant to be here… Care to tell me what?"

Simon looked at Albert's shrewd expression and nodded. If they were going to find out anything more, they needed to trust this odd little man with his blue overalls and funny contraptions.

"A sword," he said. "I'll get it."

He slipped down into the cellar, brought up the sword, and placed it on the table.

"Well now," said Albert, impressed. "There's quite a bit of workmanship in this little beauty. That's not just any old sword… An interesting thing to have come through and no mistake."

"What do you mean, *come through*?" said Cat. "Come through from where? We showed it to Mum, and she said the sword used to be our dad's."

Albert Jemmet's expression didn't change, but his blue eyes suddenly looked more alert, and Simon could tell that he had become very interested. He pointed his toothpick at Cat.

"Your dad's," he said lightly. "Really? That would be Irene's nephew, then?"

Cat nodded and Albert chewed his toothpick thoughtfully for a moment.

"You know," he said conversationally, "I thought we just had an ordinary rift on our hands to start with. And it might still be. Even with the sword. A big one, but then you do get things like that occasionally… But now there's Smith and Jones stalking about, which is not a good sign."

He looked at Simon and Cat with a frown.

"And then there's you two. Something a bit odd about you… Not surprising, really, given your great-aunt, but still. And energy readings are off the scale around the whole house. Is there anything else you'd like to tell me? Anything I can help with?"

Cat hesitated. She was feeling slightly faint, as if she were standing on the edge of an abyss. Dragons in the garden? Rifts? Nothing was making sense in terms of ordinary, everyday reality.

She raised her eyebrows at Simon, who shook his head slightly – he clearly didn't want to tell Albert about the box. Cat nodded. They would just have to see what they could find out for themselves.

"Look, Mr Jemmet," she said, in her taking-charge voice. "Thanks for the eggs, and the fumigation and all. But we're really not sure what you're talking about, and I probably ought to phone Mum to check that she did ask you to come round and, well, maybe you'd better go, we need to be getting ready for school."

Albert Jemmet smiled at her serious face.

"All right, young lady. I don't want to confuse you too much. I'll just say this. You've a bad case of electrical energies gone haywire here, and I'm guessing there's something else in the house that might explain it. Because the one thing that can

set off those sort of energies is deep amber…
and I'm beginning to wonder if that's what you've
got here. A piece of deep amber."

He looked hard at Simon, who shrugged.
"Never heard of it," he said. "What does it look
like?"

Albert Jemmet went back to chewing on
his toothpick.

"Dark yellow-orange stone," he said, watching
Simon carefully. "Probably locked up safely in
a box."

Simon, in the most neutral voice he could
muster, said, "Well, I don't think I've seen anything
like that, but I'll look out for it, I promise."

"You do that," said Albert, looking at him
with his piercing blue eyes. "And let me know
when you find it. Dangerous stuff, deep amber.
Really very dangerous. Not for those who don't
know what they're doing."

He got up, and put the fumigator away in his
capacious canvas bag.

"I'll let myself out. Just do your doors for you
first – should stop any more pest problems."

He pulled a small packet out of his bag, and
scattered a little white powder on the floor in

front of the back door, then headed down the hallway and did the same at the front door. They followed him out, and as he put the packet back in his bag they thought they heard him muttering some strange foreign-sounding words. But then he looked up, touched his forehead in a quick salute and grinned.

"All sorted for you now. No more infestations, guaranteed for a month. Don't forget to call me if you have any worries, or if you find that deep amber. *Especially* if you find the deep amber..."

He waved, and shut the door with a huge bang, which made the glass rattle.

Cat turned to her younger brother.

"Was he... was he doing a *spell*?"

Simon grinned. "It sounded like it, didn't it?"

Cat shook her head. "This is mad," she said. "I don't know what to think any more."

They returned to the kitchen, where Cat sat down rather heavily at the table and put her face in her hands.

"Deep amber," she said after a few minutes. "Do you think that's what's in the box?"

"Yes," Simon answered, "I think it must be."

There was a pause, while they thought about it.

Then Cat sat up, took a deep breath, and seemed to gather herself together.

"We need to get it open," she said. "And I think those symbols are a clue. You see if you can find anything about them on the internet at school today – I'm going to grab one of Mum's books to take with me. I suddenly realised this morning where I'd seen symbols like those before – it was in that big blue book in her study."

Leaving Simon in the kitchen she set off purposefully down the hall to the room their mother used as a study. Once inside the small boxroom, she pulled a large faded dark-blue book from one of the overstuffed bookshelves. It had a gold sun embossed on the front cover and the title, in faded gold lettering, was: *Ancient Runes and Symbols of the Lost Age*.

Chapter Seven

The Great Forest was silent and still except for a few leaves that fluttered to the ground. All Dora could see was the splintered fingers of broken trees reaching up out of the trampled undergrowth. Had the creature thrown Jem aside before her spell had turned it small? Had she somehow magicked both of them to another place entirely? Or had Jem managed to scarper into the nearby bushes?

Dora moved tentatively towards the spot where Jem had stood. When she got there it soon became clear that, whatever her spell had done to the monster, it had certainly worked a treat on Jem. He was standing in the middle of the path with his hands on his hips, looking extremely cross, and he was approximately the height of a dandelion.

"Are you all right?" said Dora, anxiously,

kneeling next to him on the path.

"Apart from being extremely short, do you mean?" said Jem, rolling his eyes. "Yes, I'm fine. But if you could see your way to restoring me to my proper height, that would be marvellous. Or better still," he added, brightening, "a hand's width taller."

"What happened to the monster?" said Dora, looking around. There was no sign of any creature, small or large.

"It disappeared," said Jem. "Just before you blasted me with your wretched spell. It just winked out. Maybe it wasn't actually real in the first place."

Dora looked doubtfully round at the flattened bushes and the torn branches of nearby trees that were now sticking out in all directions.

"It must have been real. Look at the way it's smashed the trees."

"Well – anytime you feel like turning me back to my proper height…" said Jem. "Sometime this year would be nice."

Dora gave Jem a hard stare. She was tempted just to leave him small. But she dutifully raised her arms and pointed at him, saying the words of the reversal spell.

Nothing happened.

She frowned, and tried again, but still nothing happened. She tried to look as if she'd meant this all along, and adjusted the magic a tweak to account for the rather frantic casting of the spell in the first place. But it was no good. Jem was completely unchanged.

"What?" he said, as he saw her expression. "Is there a problem?"

The crease between Dora's eyebrows deepened.

Jem looked at her sternly. "Are you saying you can't do it?"

Dora hesitated, then she said, "I'm sorry, Jem. I think it's because I was a bit rushed. I must have put a strange twist in the magic, and I can't seem to unravel it."

Jem looked at her in silence for a full minute. Dora felt as if she were the one who'd been shrunk.

"Wonderful," he said eventually. "Stuck in the middle of the Great Forest with any number of dangerous creatures, and no bigger than a frog. Brilliant work, Dora. Remind me never to go on a trip with you ever again. You're the worst witch since mad Maud Appleby turned all the castle cows into snails. At least *she* managed to turn them back again. Now I'm going to have to travel in your pocket till we find a *real* magic user who can turn me back."

Dora stopped looking apologetic and went red in the face. If Jem hadn't been so tiny she'd have punched him. All her frustration at being forced along a non-existent path thanks to Jem's stupid decision, and having to follow him through a forest that seemed less and less like a real solid place with every step, just burst out in one big rush.

"Well, I'm very sorry you've been shrunk, Mister High and Mighty Escort, but I never wanted you along in the first place, and it's thanks to your stupid decision we're here in the middle of nowhere with whatever it was charging us, and how was I to know it would just disappear of its own accord? You're *lucky* to be small and not actually dead! And if you think you're travelling in *my* pocket, you can think again!"

They glared at each other, and then, to Dora's surprise, Jem laughed, and looked a little shame-faced.

"OK. Maybe you're right, it *was* my fault we took the wrong path. I'm sorry. And you did try and save my life. So… thanks." He grinned at

Dora, and thumped her on the knee. "You know, you can be quite fierce when you decide to be." His tone was rather admiring. "I tell you what – lift me up on your shoulder and then at least I'll be able to see where we're going. I dare say we'll find someone in the city who can turn me back."

Dora took a deep breath. Wasn't that just typical of Jem. She'd finally got angry with him – and he seemed to like her better for it!

Dora grinned, and decided that she was not going to take any of Jem's nonsense any more. Especially now that he barely came up to the top of her boots.

She bent down to lift Jem up, but as she did so, something small and blue fluttered into sight. It settled on a tree branch close to her head and folded away its wings. Without them, it looked like a furry blue caterpillar.

"Sorry I'm so late," it said, not sounding the least bit sorry. "Took me for ever to find you. You've been dipping in and out of the real forest, that's the trouble."

Dora blinked, and looked again, but the blue caterpillar was still there, looking faintly put upon.

"Umm…" was all she could say, before the

caterpillar waved an imperious antenna at her.

"Caractacus at your service. Forest agent. You've got yourselves deep into the wrong bit – so they sent me to sort you out. But as I said, it's taken a while. Wherever you go, bits of other worlds keep getting mixed up all around you."

"Other worlds?" said Jem, looking up eagerly from Dora's shoulder.

The caterpillar gave him a disapproving stare. "It's the objects you've got in your packs. They're pulling things in and out of this world – probably trying to get back where they came from. And this close to the World Tree, things are always a bit mixed up."

Dora could see Jem already had his mouth open to ask another question, and she glanced sideways at him with a frown. Sir Mortimer had told them not to discuss the objects with anyone. But Jem was far too curious to care about Sir Mortimer's instructions.

"Where did the objects come from, then?" he said.

"Dear me, boy," said Caractacus with a sigh. "Use your head. One of the other worlds. It stands to reason. They're not from here, after all – where else did you think they would be from?" Caractacus shook his head, as if he couldn't quite believe how ignorant Jem was. Then he nodded at Dora's pack. "I imagine you're taking them to the palace."

Dora hesitated. They were not supposed to talk about where they were going either – but Caractacus seemed to already know about the objects, and it was generally a good idea to stay on the right side of any of the forest folk.

"The Druid said we should take them to Lord Ravenglass," she said. "Umm – sir."

"The Druid, eh?" said Caractacus. "So that's where you're from. I think maybe we'd better all sit down and have a little talk."

He slipped off his branch and flew down to sit on the ground next to them. Dora blinked. Now he was closer, he still appeared to be some kind of blue caterpillar, but he was somehow bigger, and his face was slightly more human-looking. He gestured with one of his legs, and immediately a warm, friendly little fire burst into life in front of them. An orange glow filled the clearing, and the darkness of the forest seemed to recede. He gestured again, and a basket appeared filled with bread, cheese, sweet red apples and a bottle of water.

Jem whooped. "Food! I'm starving. Let me at it."

He scrambled up into the basket and headed straight for a piece of cheese the size of his head. Just before he started to get his teeth into it, he turned to Caractacus.

"So you're a forest agent? What's one of those, then?"

Caractacus put his head on one side, as if considering how much to tell Jem.

"The forest agents keep the worlds stable," he said, eventually. "There are many worlds, and they all originate here. They're part of the World Tree. We look after the balance of those worlds, deal with any problems that come up." He snorted. "Of course, this particular agent is meant to be *retired*. Four hundred years of service – you'd think it would be enough. But no – you two come blundering in, pulling the energies every which way, and suddenly everyone else is just too busy to deal with it."

He picked up a long green stem and began to chew it absently. "Of course, now I'm here, I can see that it's just as well it was me that came. I'd better contact our agent in that world. We may have a serious rift developing, and that would mean there's deep amber at the bottom of it."

"Deep amber?" said Dora. She had a feeling she'd heard the words before, somewhere.

Caractacus looked at Dora, and sighed. "Don't you know *anything*?" he said. "Maybe I'd better begin at the beginning. Get yourself something to eat before the boy finishes it all off, and I'll tell you both the story of the forest, and the World Tree, and all the worlds."

He settled himself against the tree trunk he was leaning on, stretched out his multiple legs, and took a deep breath. As he spoke, the firelight dimmed, and the green shadows of the forest grew closer.

"In the beginning, there was nothing but snow and ice and darkness, and in this darkness lived the wolves and ice giants, the shape-shifters, the crow karls and creatures of the dark."

Dora shivered. She could almost see the cold waste, and the dark creatures roaming across it. And now that Caractacus had started, she knew she'd heard this story before, from her grandfather. It was the story of how the world began.

"Then," Caractacus said, with a little flick of

one of his feet, "a small crack appeared in the ice, and light flowed from it like a river. A little plant pushed its way out of the crack, and this plant grew until it became a great tree, gathering light and warmth and life around it."

Dora gasped as the fire seemed to glow more brightly, and a little finger of flame rose up from it into the air. A shimmering tree shape grew out of the flame, right in front of them. It got bigger and bigger and branches started to spread out from it.

Caractacus continued in a low voice, and as he spoke, they could see the story unfold in front of them in the fire.

"The surrounding lands became warm and bright and full of other trees. The first humans appeared, along with the first dwarves and elves and other magic folk, and they all sheltered under the Tree and lived in the forest around it. As the Tree grew tall, other worlds grew from it, like fruit from its spreading branches, and humans and others learned to travel freely between all the worlds. Everywhere the ice and darkness was pushed back."

The scene in front of Dora and Jem was beautiful. There were tiny creatures flitting around the tree in the spreading forest, and on each branch they could see misty worlds in which were more tiny people. But then at the edges the scene suddenly started to darken, and tendrils of shadows started to invade the picture.

"But at the edges of the worlds, the shape-shifters and wolves, the dark crow karls and the ice giants remained. The creatures of darkness were jealous of the warmth and life of the worlds," said Caractacus sadly, "and they wanted to destroy the Tree and the worlds it sheltered so that everything would become cold and dark once more. Over the years they tried many ways to invade the worlds and harm the Tree – but the forest folk, with those of the humans who had some magic, gathered together to protect the Tree, and with it the balance of the worlds. So far they have always succeeded in pushing back the forces of the dark."

He made a gesture with a few of his feet, and the images faded. Then he blinked at them both. "So that's the forest agents – they watch over the worlds, and push back the dark wherever it tries to gain a foothold."

There was a silence, the dimness that had

surrounded them lifted, and then the fire started to crackle again.

"My grandfather used to tell a story a bit like that," said Dora, slowly. "I'd forgotten it till now… About the heroes who travelled to different worlds and fought the creatures of darkness. But the creatures of darkness don't exist, do they?"

Caractacus looked grim. "Oh, they exist all right. Although we've been mercifully untroubled by them for a long time. However, it's always best to be on your guard."

"Was that monster that attacked us – was that a creature of darkness?" asked Jem, sounding slightly awed.

Caractacus nearly choked with laughter. "No, no! That was an elephant. A creature from the world your objects come from. The objects have been pulling the energies around, like I said, pulling you and other things back and forth between the forest and their world. I wonder…"

He hesitated for a moment, and then seemed to come to a decision. He briskly waved the little fire and food into non-existence.

"I was still eating that!" objected Jem loudly. Caractacus rolled his eyes.

"Pick the boy up," he said to Dora. "I think it's time we were getting you to the other side of the forest. This rift is serious and I'm almost certain there's amber at the bottom of it. There's an agent I can contact in that world, but it might be as well to get word to the palace, too. I'll escort you, and make sure no more elephants turn up."

He twisted slightly and unfurled his wings again, hovering by Dora's head.

"Come along," he said. "This way."

It took less than ten minutes for Caractacus to guide them back to the path, although Dora was convinced they'd travelled quite considerably further than it seemed. The trees slid past them in a disconcerting way and quite often it felt as if a single step had taken them to a different part of the forest entirely. When they reached the path, Caractacus settled down on a branch, and yawned loudly.

"Off you go then," he said. "Not too far from here to the edge of the forest, and you can pick up a cart ride to the city from the first village you get to."

Dora bobbed a curtsy. "Thank you, your – er – magnificence," she said.

The caterpillar graciously inclined his head.

"Um – any chance you could turn me back to the right size before we go on?" asked Jem hopefully.

Caractacus squinted at him. "You look fine to me," he said. "Very useful, being small, I find. It suits you. I'd stay that way if I were you." And he rolled up into a very final-looking ball and went to sleep.

"Rats," said Jem. "Suppose I'll be stuck this way till we get to the palace then. But still – Dora – other worlds! The things we've got come from *another world*! Do you think we could go there somehow? I wonder how you become a forest agent?"

But Dora wasn't listening. She had suddenly remembered the letter of introduction to Lord Ravenglass – the letter that they needed to get into the palace. It was in Jem's pack – and Jem's pack was now no bigger than her thumbnail. Dora's insides felt as if they were plummeting into a deep hole, as she realised that the letter of introduction would now be approximately the size of an apple pip, and any writing on it would be completely impossible to decipher.

Chapter Eight

"Got it!" said Cat, slapping her hand down on the book of symbols.

"Got what?" said Simon, startled.

It was the morning after Albert Jemmet's fumigation, and it was an inset day, so Mum was at work. The two of them were huddled in Simon's bedroom, and working hard on the box problem. The internet had proved less than useful for information on how to get into the box – apart from anything else, Simon had complained, how do you type a symbol into Google? And even when he'd tried to describe them, he'd just ended up with tons of weird stuff on crystal healing or people who acted out Viking battles in their spare time.

But Cat had been luckier. She had spent

every spare minute studying the book of ancient symbols, and comparing them to careful copies she had made of the symbols on the wooden box. Now she was sitting on the floor of Simon's bedroom, the big book open in front of her, and her eyes were shining.

"I went through the whole book twice," she said. "And I realised something… Each symbol on the box is actually a combination of symbols – there's a Norse rune and two alchemical symbols. This first one has the rune for fire just below the alchemical symbol meaning *dissolve* – and they're both surrounded by the alchemical symbol for water. So I think that means we have to surround the box in water that has fire dissolved in it."

Simon raised one eyebrow. "Dissolved *fire*? As in…?"

Cat waved her hands excitedly. "I know, it sounded ridiculous to me, too, at first. But I think what it's saying is to immerse it in a kind of liquid fire…"

She looked at Simon expectantly, but he shrugged, bemused.

"Think of Christmas puddings," she said, encouragingly.

"*Christmas puddings?*" he said. "Um – are you sure you're feeling all right, Cat?"

She grinned. "I'm feeling like a genius," she said. "Because that's what I am. When you pour brandy all over a Christmas pudding and then set light to it, what happens?"

"Er... Not sure... It burns, I guess..." Suddenly Simon's face cleared. "Of course! The brandy is liquid, but it flames if you set it alight... So the pudding is surrounded by *water that has fire dissolved in it!* Wow! Do you really think that's it?"

"I think it's worth a try," said Cat. "Maybe the heat is what unlocks part of the mechanism inside the box. And then there are obviously two more things you have to do, which look like mixtures of symbols too. Now I know how the first one works, I should be able to get the other two quite easily."

Simon took the book, and leafed through a few pages, looking back and forth between the symbols and Cat's drawing. She was right, the first symbol on the box was a combination of the Norse rune for fire and a curly shape at the top that looked like the sign for dissolving, inside the alchemy triangle that stood for water. The other symbols looked like they would be the same. He traced his finger over them thoughtfully. Despite Cat's attempt at a sensible explanation, he didn't think she really believed there was a simple heat-sensitive mechanism inside the box. The sword had come from the *other side*, Jemmet had said, and that meant the box probably had, too. Appearances, disappearances, strange energies – none of it fitted into the ordinary world of locks and bolts.

Simon passed Cat the book of runes and leaned back on his pillow. There was something he'd been wanting to say for ages, but he was afraid Cat would think it was ridiculous. The sword that had appeared was definitely their dad's – Mum had said so, and she should know. Besides, there was something about it that felt deeply right, like a puzzle piece that fitted exactly into a blank space. But the sword was also somehow mixed up with something that Simon was pretty sure was magic, not 'electrical energy' or 'radiation'. And all of it came back, in the end, to Dad.

Simon hadn't thought about his dad much, before now. He'd seen pictures of him, knew about who he was, what he'd done, but he only had the faintest memories. Since the sword had arrived, though, Simon had experienced a strong sense of his dad's presence – the smell of him, the feel of him, the bristly chin when he'd picked Simon up to kiss him goodnight. Suddenly, Simon had found for the first time that he *missed* him, properly, as a person he'd known, but who wasn't there any more. And that had made Simon wonder – if there was magic in the world, and if his dad was connected to it, could it be possible that...

Simon propped himself up on his elbow.

"Cat," he said, hesitantly. "Do you think... Could it be that... Could Dad be alive, somewhere? Could he... could he have sent the sword from this other side that Albert Jemmet was talking about?"

Cat looked up from tracing another rune, shocked. "Alive?" she said. "But – how could he be alive?"

She was right, thought Simon, it was a crazy idea, but he ploughed on anyway.

"Well, maybe he came from this other world, maybe he had to go there for some reason and couldn't come back... So he sent us his sword..."

Cat shook her head in disbelief. "Simon – that's just mad! You can't seriously believe Dad might be alive and in another world?"

Simon sighed. "Oh, I don't know – I guess not. But it just seemed... you know? Odd. The sword was his, and then it just appears..."

Cat gave him a sympathetic look, and reached over to gently pat him on the knee. "I wish Dad was alive, too, you know. But there was definitely nothing strange about him. He was a bit crazy, and into all that medieval stuff, but so are lots of people. Mum is! It doesn't mean they're from some... other world. And he definitely died. I remember it – the funeral and everything."

Simon sighed. She was probably right. But then *someone* had to be responsible for all the odd things that had started happening.

"What about Great-Aunt Irene, then?" he said. "We found all this stuff in her house, after all. And she was a bit weird."

"She was completely nuts," said Cat. "But that doesn't mean she came from another world either. Besides, she'd lived in this house *for ever*. She must have been from here."

"Oh!" said Simon, throwing himself back on

his pillow in frustration. "I don't know! Maybe they're *all* from another world. Great-Aunt Irene, Dad, Uncle Lou – the whole town!"

"Or maybe no one is," said Cat, firmly. She threw him half a chocolate bar she'd dug out of her school bag. "Because there *aren't* any other worlds, and magic doesn't *exist*."

Simon shrugged, and munched his chocolate slowly, watching Cat bend in concentration over the book of runes once again. They seemed to be getting nowhere.

"Maybe you're right," he said. "Maybe it really is just some electrical fault and a few strange coincidences, and Albert Jemmet's just a bit mad... Hey, Cat?"

But Cat wasn't listening, because she'd suddenly worked out what the second combination of symbols meant.

"Ice!" she said. "It's ice. Water that's solidified! Oh, yes! I am *totally* a genius! And it's inside the symbol for earth... We can use some soil from the garden!"

The kitchen was full of smoke, and the smoke alarm was beeping fit to bust. Cat waved a magazine in front of it while Simon wrenched open the back door, and after a few more seconds of ear-splitting beeps, the alarm subsided.

Cat had finally worked out the last lot of symbols, "It's the rune for fire inside air, and the other symbol says it has to be projected, so I think that means a fiery wind. We can use my hairdryer on the hot setting..."

They had decided to try and open the box immediately, and the kitchen table had seemed the safest place for experimenting.

Simon and Cat looked at the wooden box, lying in the centre of a baking tray on the kitchen table. It seemed untouched. The ceiling, meanwhile, had several sooty scorch marks.

"I said a splash," said Cat. "Not half the bottle."

Simon made an apologetic face. "I thought it had to be surrounded. I didn't realise the flames would go that high. Just as well Mum's not here."

"Right," said Cat, who was still wearing her dressing gown. "Ice inside earth next."

Simon reached out for the plastic box full of ice cubes that they'd decanted from the freezer, and poured them on top of the box so that they covered it completely, then plonked a pile of garden soil on top and patted it down.

"How long do you think we wait?" he said.

Cat glanced at the clock. "Let's give it five minutes, " she suggested. "It should cool it down enough to do whatever it's supposed to do." She leaned close to the box. "I wonder if we'll hear a click or something."

Simon looked sceptical. He was certain this was nothing to do with heating or cooling the lock. They were trying to do something much more complicated, something more sideways and possibly even magical.

After five minutes, they dug the box out of the ice and soil. It looked exactly the same, apart from a few muddy smears. Cat picked up her hair dryer and turning it to full blast on maximum heat, pointed it right at the box.

Simon wasn't sure what he had expected to happen. The lid to fly open, perhaps? Some startling change of colour, or sparks?

But the box stayed exactly the same. When Simon reached out to try the lid, it was just as firmly locked as it was to start with. He looked at Cat, who shrugged.

And then, at that precise moment, he heard

a querulous voice saying quite distinctly, "Oh do get on with it. You are quite hopeless!"

"Did you hear that?' he asked Cat, who had turned quite white.

"Yes," she said, shakily. "It… it sounded like it was coming from the box."

Simon thought so too. But what was even stranger was that the voice had sounded extraordinarily like Great-Aunt Irene.

Chapter Nine

The Druid had been having a trying couple of days. He'd spent the morning of Dora and Jem's departure battling a fire at the mill which had turned out to be the work of a rather troublesome dragon, and required quite a quantity of magic to defeat it. It didn't help that he'd mislaid his sword somewhere, and had been forced to borrow Sir Roderick's, which didn't have anything like as good a balance. Then, when he'd finally returned to the castle, he had been greeted by the sight of all the squires' undergarments fluttering in the breeze from the top of the battlements. Somehow, Jem had managed to continue his feud with the castle squires without even being there. Sir Mortimer was furious, and the squires were demanding that Jem be banished without trial. All of which took some time and energy to smooth over.

So it wasn't until the day after Dora and Jem had set out for the city that the Druid heard from Sir Mortimer about the third strange object.

"A third? *Another?* Are you sure?"

"Ah… erm… yes. Sorry. I did mean to tell you on the day, but what with one thing and another… It was a little red box – Jem found it. Was it important?"

The Druid sighed. "Well, yes. If there are three, it means it's almost certainly the amber at the bottom of it. Someone will need to get it under control." He ran his hands through his hair. "I can't go," he said at last. "I promised I wouldn't interfere."

"Umm, very good," said Sir Mortimer, trying to look as if he understood what the Druid was talking about. "Shall I – er – order the castle on high alert?"

"No – I don't think so," said the Druid, looking more cheerful. "Dora and Jem will be at the city by now. Lord Ravenglass will deal with it – or the forest folk. Someone will sort it out."

The city was a jumble of alleyways and broad streets, each full of inns and houses, carts and animal pens, hawkers and stalls selling everything you could imagine. Dora and Jem were dropped off just inside the city walls after a rattling cart ride from the edge of the forest. Neither of them had ever seen so many people in one place, even at the Summer Fair, which was busy enough for anyone as far as Dora was concerned. And there was a ripe, tangy smell everywhere of animals and market produce and rotting vegetables and cooking.

Dora was sure she was going to get robbed or lost as soon as she passed through the city gate, but most people seemed to just ignore her, and the palace was not exactly difficult to spot. It towered above the rest of the city, with glimpses of the white turrets visible from almost every street corner. But finding the streets that went in the direction of the palace and didn't end in tiny smelly courtyards or high walls around some noble's garden proved more tricky. Especially with Jem constantly shouting contradictory directions in her ear, trying to be heard over the rattle of carts on the cobblestones or the creak of market stalls being dismantled or the squeal of pigs being driven off to new quarters.

Finally, however, they made it safely to the palace, just before the gates shut for the night. Now they would have to persuade the palace guards to let them in, and that, Dora thought, was not going to be easy.

The gate guards wore purple velvet tunics liberally festooned with gold braid, and they carried ceremonial spears that gleamed gold in the last of the sunshine and were about twice the height of Dora. The palace itself rose up behind them, with endless high white stone walls and the hint of turrets and battlements only partly visible from the narrow cobbled street they were in.

The chief guard, who had several extra bits of gold braid attached to his tunic, looked at them with disdain.

"Yes?" he said, in a not very encouraging voice.

"Umm… if you please, sir, we – I – have come to see Lord Ravenglass, with a message," said Dora.

The guard looked her up and down and sniffed loudly.

"Letter of introduction?" he said, holding out his hand.

Dora fished out Jem's tiny pack from her pocket. She tipped out the small object that she was pretty sure was the letter of introduction, and held out her hand with it nestled in the middle of her palm.

The guard looked at her as if she were mad, and then bent over to peer at the object.

"That's not a letter of introduction, that's a speck of dust," he said. "What good do you think that's going to do?"

Dora started to try and explain about the forest and the monster and the spell to turn things small – but the guard wasn't interested.

"No letter of introduction, no entrance to the palace. Now clear off and stop wasting my time."

He went back to his position opposite the other guard, and they clanged their spears together across the entrance, their faces stern and unmoving.

"But we have to see Lord Ravenglass. There *must* be a way to get an appointment with him!" said Dora, desperately.

The chief guard looked down at her as if she were a slug about to eat his prize lettuce.

"Lord Ravenglass is a Courtier of the First Degree," he said in an exasperated voice. "He can only be approached by a Courtier of the Second Degree, and then only on Tuesdays between eleven and twelve. To petition a Courtier of the Second Degree, you need the favour of a Third Degree nobleman. You can apply to *them* for an appointment, via the Under-Secretary of the Steward's Office, by making an application in advance. Current waiting time is three weeks." And he clashed his spear back across the palace entrance in a very final manner.

It was lucky that the money Sir Mortimer had given them was in Dora's pack and not Jem's. It meant that at least they had full-size coins to pay for a meal and a room for the night at one of the city's less grubby inns.

Dora had felt rather nervous asking for a room for the night, but the landlady had taken pity on the lost-looking girl with the dark plaits and worried frown, and had bundled Dora straight upstairs to a quiet room at the back of the inn. She and Jem were now sitting by a warm fire, finishing off the remains of food from their packs and trying to figure out what to do next. Their meeting with Caractacus had left both of them with the feeling that there was something quite seriously odd going on, and that their message to the palace might be more urgent than either of them had thought.

"Do you think it's true?" said Jem, picking at a piece of chicken bone as long as his arm. "Other worlds, and the creatures of the dark and all that? Do you think these objects really do come from another world?"

Dora nodded. "They feel like it," she said. "And the Druid said that they were. He wanted the palace to know so they could do something about it. And that was when he thought there were only two. From what Caractacus said, three is even more serious."

"I wish we could go there," said Jem, dreamily. "To the other world. Maybe we could help. Maybe they'll ask us to go… What do you think, Dora?"

"I think we need to worry about getting into the palace first," said Dora, firmly. "That's what we were sent here for, and unless we get the message to Lord Ravenglass, no one's going to be doing *anything* to help."

Jem nodded, and they returned to thinking of ways to get past the gate guards.

It was midnight before they were close to a plan, and even then it was one Dora was not at all happy about.

"Look, it's fine," said Jem, exasperated. "I'll slip past the gate guards while you ask them some question or other, and then I'll just sneak around the palace till I find Lord Ravenglass. No one will see me."

"But anything could happen!" objected Dora. "You could get stepped on. Or eaten by a dog. Or – anything! It's too dangerous!"

Jem rolled his eyes. "You're so *wet*, Dora! It's an adventure! It's a chance for a bit of glory!"

Dora snorted. "What – so you can show off to your friends when we get back? So you can impress Violet Wetherby with your daring?"

Jem frowned. "Violet Wetherby? Why in all the kingdom would I want to impress *her*?"

"I thought you – well, she said all those things when we were leaving. About you bringing her back a present," said Dora, confused.

Jem made a face. "Violet Wetherby is a flibbertigibbet and a nasty piece of work besides," he said firmly. "I wouldn't bring her back a *slug*, not even if she begged me on bended knees."

"Really?" said Dora, feeling absurdly pleased.

"Of course!" said Jem. "Honestly – Violet Wetherby? Please! And now can we agree that I ought to sneak into the palace? After all, it's your fault I'm smaller than a dandelion. I ought at least to get a chance to do something that makes it worthwhile."

Dora hesitated, then nodded.

"All right. Maybe it is the only way. We'll go back to the palace first thing in the morning. But Jem – you'll need to be careful! And if you don't get anywhere by midday, just come back to the gate – I'll wait for you there."

"Don't look so worried, Dora," said Jem, grinning. "It'll be easy. Lord Ravenglass will probably be so impressed he'll make me a knight on the spot!"

Several hours later, crouching in a shadow by the corner of a tapestry, Jem was wondering if Dora had been right after all. Finding his way through the palace when he was smaller than a weed and couldn't ask directions was turning out to be a bit like trying to find your way through the Great Forest with objects from another world in your pack – difficult, dangerous and likely to end badly. So far he'd managed to avoid being stepped on, but it had been a close call a couple of times.

Jem peered out from behind the tapestry at the legs passing swiftly past him. He seemed to be in a passage somewhere near the kitchens – a large number of brightly liveried servants were hurrying to and fro with plates and trays, and there was a strong smell of food. Unfortunately, there was also a faint sound of dogs barking, and Jem had a nasty feeling it was getting closer. He crept further along the passageway, trying to keep to the shadows. He had no idea what time it was, but it must be getting near midday. He thought of Dora, sitting outside the castle gates waiting for him, and wondered if he'd ever see her again.

Suddenly, he froze. The sound of barking was now much, much closer. It sounded like several dogs, all chasing each other, and he was pretty sure they were all heading straight this way.

Jem looked behind him, and swore. At least three hounds were tearing down the passage, snapping at each other's heels, and one of them had already knocked a servant flying. A large silver platter was somersaulting Jem's way, and various bits of meat and pastries were heading in every direction around it.

Jem did the only thing he could think of – he ran. Down the passageway, avoiding the bits of flying food, dodging in between the running legs and hoping the yelps he could hear behind him were the dogs getting what they deserved from the angry swarm of servants. He spotted an archway to his left and sprinted through it, only to run straight into what seemed like a wall of solid grey cloth.

"Aaargh!" came a shriek from above him, and he stumbled backwards, almost losing his balance. "A mouse! In my skirts… It's a… No, it's a… Aaarggh! It's *horrible!*"

Nuts, thought Jem. It's a *girl*. Must be one of the kitchen maids or something. He looked round swiftly for somewhere to hide but the room was quite bare, except for a few buckets in one corner and some boxes of vegetables. Jem dived head first into a pile of lettuces and burrowed down as far as he could – but it sounded like the girl's shrieks had brought a search party.

"Where's the nasty thing?" came a deeper voice, as the box Jem was in was shifted across the floor so they could look behind it. "I'll not have creatures in my kitchen. Fetch Fred!"

Jem kept as still as he could and hoped Fred was short-sighted. But his luck wasn't in. Fred, it turned out, was a dog – and he had a very good sense of smell. It wasn't long before he was scratching at the box where Jem was hiding, and his snuffling whining muzzle was very close indeed to Jem's head.

Then a meaty hand reached into the box, and Jem was grabbed by the hair and pulled out of the lettuces.

"Urgh!" said the deep voice. "It's a dirty stable boy, magicked smaller than a duckling. That'll be those pesky apprentice wizards again. Put the lad in a cupboard somewhere safe. He's evidence. I'm going to have their guts this time!"

Jem waved his legs wildly and yelled, "I'm not a stable boy. I've got a message. For Lord Ravenglass. It's important! He'll be *furious* if you put me in a cupboard!"

The voice raised Jem up to its face, and Jem saw that it was large, and red, with a bristling black moustache. He had a feeling both voice and face probably belonged to the chief cook.

"Lord Ravenglass, eh?" said the red-faced man with a deep chuckle. "Well, then, better take you up to his Lordship immediately. But I hope for your sake your message is important, boy. Because Lord Ravenglass has got a nasty temper, and a lot of magic. You might find worse happening to you than being put in a cupboard!"

Chapter Ten

Simon was bored. Cat was now completely focused on working out how to get into the box, and she didn't want his help. She was sitting at the kitchen table, still in her dressing-gown and pyjamas, with her head bent over the book of ancient symbols. Every time Simon tried to say anything, she waved him away crossly.

Simon eventually gave up and wandered into the living room. But then he thought about the sword, tucked away safely in the cellar. He had been aching to get hold of it again ever since it had been removed and firmly put away. He had a feeling the sword was as much of a clue to what was going on as the box. With Mum away and Cat distracted, now seemed like a very good opportunity to take a better look at it.

Simon crept carefully to the cellar, gently took the sword down from the shelf it was lying on, and tiptoed back to the living room. He weighed the sword in his hand, then took it by the handle and tried a few preliminary sweeps through the air. It made a very satisfactory swishing sound.

Simon adjusted his stance, moving his feet slightly further apart and clasping the sword firmly in both hands. There was something about the weight and smoothness of the hilt that just seemed completely right, as if the sword were an extension of his arm. He swept the sword diagonally down, and then quickly reversed his grip and brought it across his body, imagining it clanging against the shield of an armoured opponent. He made a few swift passes, back and forth. Then he raised it above his head, and brought it swiftly downwards onto an imaginary opponent's shield.

The sword sliced through the arm of the sofa with a wrenching, splitting sound that travelled right down the hall and into the kitchen. Simon, horrified at what he'd done, looked up to see Cat standing in the doorway with her arms folded, eyebrows raised.

"You do realise Mum's going to kill you, don't you?" she said, in a matter-of-fact voice.

"Umm… yes," said Simon, wondering how many weeks' pocket-money would be enough to pay for a sofa. He tried to pick the sofa arm up and stick it back in the right place. It stayed there for a heartbeat, but then it sagged and toppled to the ground again, a forlorn dribble of stuffing spilling out onto the carpet.

"Lovely," said Cat. "Maybe you'd better put the sword back where it belongs – in the cellar."

"Mmm," said Simon and followed her back to the kitchen, but despite the damage he'd done, he had no intention of putting the sword back. There had been something that nagged at the corner of his brain as he used it – he needed to try it out again so he could work out what it was. As Cat settled back in front of the rune book, he banged the cellar door as if he'd gone down there, and then waited quietly for a couple of minutes. When she seemed thoroughly absorbed, he slipped past her and into the garden, the sword hidden behind his back.

The sun was shining, and there was a line of washing strung from the back of the house across the garden to the old beech tree in the corner, moving slightly as it was lifted by the occasional gust of wind. Simon found a clear space between the garden wall and the washing line and tightly gripped the sword again. He closed his eyes, and imagined himself in the middle of a roaring crowd, fully armoured, a dark figure with sword raised.

He made a few tentative passes, imagining an enemy walking towards him with a heavy tread. Then he opened his eyes and swung the sword up into the air, the sunlight glinting off the shining length of metal. He felt a huge burst of exhilaration – it was as if he could really hear the roars of the crowd around him as he cut and thrust and parried and gradually beat back his imaginary opponent in triumph.

Suddenly there was a harsh cry overhead, and Simon looked up, startled. A black shadow flicked across in front of him, and then he saw another flying in his direction, and another. The shadows came together to form a dense cloud of black crows wheeling across the garden, circling over his head… He thought of the crow's feather that Albert Jemmet had fumigated.

Simon was about to run, but before he could work out which direction to run in, the crows stopped circling and all of them started to dive straight for where he was standing.

Instinct kicked in. His arms came up and the sword flashed. There was a flapping and squawking, but the birds kept coming. Simon swept the big sword round his head, this way and then that, wildly whacking and slashing and whirling round as fast as he could to keep the birds at bay until, with angry cries, they all seemed to give up at the same time and flew off shrieking, leaving Simon panting and alone in the middle of the garden.

He took a deep breath and looked around. Black crow feathers were scattered across the grass, but lying among them, looking muddy and crumpled, was most of the washing that had been drying on the line when he came out. Simon's wild hacking had seen the crows off, but it had also chopped Mum's washing line and most of her washing into several pieces.

Cat was finding it hard to concentrate on the book of symbols. Every time she thought she was getting somewhere, there was another thump from the cellar. What was Simon *doing* in there? Eventually, after a resounding crash that set all the plates in the kitchen rattling, she got up with a sigh and went to the cellar door.

"What on earth do you think you're—" she began as she opened the door. And then she stopped and gulped, and stepped backwards.

Crashing up the steps out of the cellar and into the kitchen came a large white horse, and following fast behind was a man in a full suit of armour, with a sword.

He looked round rather wildly, then spotted Cat and seemed to relax. He bowed deeply.

"Most beautiful lady, you are surely a rich and powerful princess," he said, looking appreciatively at the swirling gold patterns of her dressing gown. "It must be your magic that has called me to this strange castle. I am at your service, for whatever task you summoned me for."

The knight was tall, with curling black hair and blue eyes in a deeply sunburnt face. He was, Cat thought rather distractedly, extremely handsome. She instinctively started to smooth down her hair and rearrange her dressing gown, but then she stopped and blinked. What was she thinking? The knight had just appeared out of the *cellar*. And there was a *horse* in the kitchen!

At that moment the back door banged, and Simon tumbled in, looking rather breathless and holding his sword.

The effect on the stranger was instantaneous. He leapt across the kitchen, his sword in front of him, disarmed Simon with a flick of the wrist, and had him pinned to the wall before Cat even had time to scream.

"Halt, and declare your business, miscreant knight!" commanded the stranger.

Cat grabbed the knight's arm and pulled. "What are you doing?" she said. "Leave him alone! He *lives* here!"

"Ah," said the knight, lowering his sword. "My apologies, sir. You are perhaps this most ravishing young lady's brother?" He looked questioningly at Cat, who nodded weakly. The knight sheathed his sword, and bowed.

"Gentle lady, and good sir knight," he said, "I am Sir Bedwyr. You have called me forth by your magicks, and I am bound to whatever quest comes my way in this strange land."

Cat swallowed, and waved her hand in a kind of

general greeting. Magic? Her legs felt rather weak. There seemed no point in denying it any more… there *was* magic, and there *was* another world – and it looked as if someone from that other world had just crashed right into their kitchen.

The knight turned to his horse, and gave it a pat on the shoulder. "And my gallant steed, Dappletoes, is at your service also."

"Dappletoes?" said Cat. Despite her shock, she felt a strong desire to giggle.

Sir Bedwyr coughed, and coloured slightly. "Dappletoes was given me by a lady, who bade me call him so. I have fought many knights who dared to laugh at his name," he added, with a frown at Simon. Simon was trying very hard not to explode with laughter and he looked like he might be in danger of choking as a result.

"You find the name amusing, young sir?" said Sir Bedwyr, and put his hand to his sword with a meaningful look.

"N-no, no, of course not!" said Simon, but he was very red in the face and Sir Bedwyr was starting to look tetchy, so Cat decided she had better intervene. She moved in front of Simon, and bowed slightly to the knight.

"Thank you for... er... responding to my magic," she said. "We are very pleased to meet you."

Sir Bedwyr took Cat's hand and kissed it. "My lady," he said, looking at her appreciatively. "I am at your service. But – if it would please you – a jug of mead would be most welcome after my long journey."

"Um... I'm not sure we've got any mead," said Cat, blushing at the kiss. "How about a cup of tea?"

Sir Bedwyr bowed. "Any refreshments would be most welcome, my lady. Especially from such a fair hand as yours."

It was quite hard to make tea with a large white horse in the way, especially when Sir Bedwyr insisted on showering Cat with non-stop compliments and appreciative glances, making her get all flustered and forget where the tea-bags were kept. Eventually though, the knight was happily settled at the kitchen table, slurping his tea and examining a cheese sandwich with interest, allowing Cat to manoeuvre Simon over to the corner by the window for a swift consultation.

"What do we do?" she said, in a low voice,

when they were nicely hidden behind the horse. "He's obviously from the same place as the sword. Do you think we should call Jemmet?"

"But I thought other worlds and magic didn't exist?" said Simon, with a grin.

Cat rolled her eyes. "Okay, okay – you win," she said. "Clearly they do. But should we call Jemmet? Things seem to be getting out of hand. And... oh my God! What did you do to Mum's washing?"

Her eyes had strayed out of the window to the garden, and she could see the trampled bits of laundry scattered over the muddy lawn like left-over patches of white snow after a thaw. She looked back at Simon.

"Mum is *absolutely* going to kill you," she said.

He waved his arm impatiently. "I know – I know. But right now we've got a large knight from another world sitting at the kitchen table and a white horse eating the pot plants. I'd say we've got more pressing things to worry about than washing."

Cat nodded. She contemplated Sir Bedwyr, who was now happily tucking in to the cheese sandwich, and then pulled Albert Jemmet's business card out of her dressing-gown pocket. She picked up her mobile. "Right. I'd better call—"

But at that moment, Dappletoes lifted his head and gave a loud whinny. He clattered round, sending several bits of furniture flying, and then set off up the hallway. Sir Bedwyr leapt to his feet.

"My Quest!" he said. "It's time – my noble horse has sensed something!"

"No! I mean… I'm sure it's nothing," said Cat anxiously. "Really – we need you to just stay here. We have a friend… "

But the light of battle was in Sir Bedwyr's blue eyes. "My dear lady – I must thank you for your hospitality, but you have no pressing need of my services. You have a knight of your own." He nodded at Simon. "I have been brought to this strange land for a reason – I must go and seek it, and not be distracted, even by the charming pleasures of so beautiful a lady." He winked at Cat, who blushed again.

Sir Bedwyr turned decisively, followed his horse down the hallway, and shouldered open the front door with a crash.

"Farewell! I go to seek adventure and just

rewards," he called back to them, and then leaped onto his horse and went clattering off down the road.

"We've got to stop him. He might hurt someone!" said Simon, running out after him.

Cat pulled off her dressing-gown and threw on her coat over her pyjamas. She followed Simon out, slamming the door shut and chucking him his jacket. "He's heading towards the town centre," she said. "You follow him, I'll call Albert Jemmet and catch up with you. Go on, get after him – quickly!"

Chapter Eleven

Either side of the great palace gates was a short row of simple stone benches, where those petitioning for entrance, or waiting for an appointment, could sit and rest. There was generally a straggle of less important visitors sitting there – travellers looking for a convenient place to sit and eat their lunch or city folk having a gossip – but most of them stayed for only a short time before moving on. Dora had been sitting there since before breakfast, trying not to attract attention and hoping fervently that Jem was safe and on his way out of the palace. It was well after midday now, and she had nearly given up on him ever appearing.

Suddenly there was a commotion by the gate, and a short man in a silver-braid uniform

134

strode out and called, in a surprisingly loud voice: "Dora Puddlefoot! Dora Puddlefoot is requested to attend Lord Ravenglass, at once!"

Dora jumped up, and hurried to the entrance. As she reached the gate, the servant looked her up and down as if to make sure she fitted a description he'd been given, and then set off at a brisk pace across the palace yard. Dora followed him along endless twists and turns of stone passageways and up and down winding stairs till she felt quite lost. But eventually they arrived at a richly carved oak door that was half open.

"Lord Ravenglass will see you now," said the servant, and gestured at the door. Dora took a deep breath, and sidled in, looking at her feet. When she raised her head, she saw, first of all, a roaring log fire, and then a small stool nearby, where Jem was sitting, happily restored to his natural size. Finally, her eyes fell on a portly man dressed in a great deal of velvet and lace, with a number of jewelled rings on his white hands. He was sitting in a large oak chair with his legs stretched out towards the fire.

Dora bowed. "Your Lordship," she said.

The man, who had a handsome, if slightly

jowly, face and a great deal of black hair in ringlets, waved one plump hand at her in a gesture of annoyance.

"No, no – forty-five degrees to the horizontal, for exactly four minutes," he said, petulantly. "Dancing dragons, what did they teach you at Roland Castle about manners? You are – what – a fourth- or fifth-level apprentice, and I am – let's see now – ah, yes… *the queen's nephew.* Do it *again.*"

Dora nervously bent down again in a lower bow, and stayed there for what she thought was safely four full minutes. When she straightened, Lord Ravenglass was looking altogether more friendly.

"That's better. Now come and sit down and eat something, you must be hungry." He waved his hand at a platter of bread and cheese on a small table nearby. Dora sat down nervously. She suddenly realised that she was indeed extremely hungry, but she was too nervous to do more than nibble at a small piece of bread.

Lord Ravenglass, having made his point about etiquette, was now picking at a plate of rich sweets and pastries and seemed much more cheerful. Jem, Dora noted with surprise, seemed to be largely responsible for his good humour. He was managing to stay just the right side of impertinent while also shamelessly buttering up Lord Ravenglass – this, Dora suddenly realised, must have been how Jem had managed to get away with doing whatever he wanted at Roland Castle. He was very good at being charming to people in charge.

She smiled and relaxed slightly as she listened to Jem's tale of the time he had been chased up all four towers of the castle by Sir Mortimer. The lord of the castle had finally cornered Jem in the pigsty, but as he'd lunged at the kitchen boy, Sir Mortimer had tripped over a large bucket of pig swill and gone flying. He'd spent the next four days trying to get pig slime out of the grooves in his armour.

"Well, young Jem," said Lord Ravenglass indulgently, still giggling slightly at the image of Sir Mortimer covered in swill, "I'm glad to hear you're keeping things lively in the far reaches of the kingdom. But now we'd better have a look at these… objects that have been appearing. I believe your friend has them?"

Dora nodded, and dug out Jem's miniature pack. With a wave of his hand, Lord Ravenglass restored it to the proper size. She took out the red fortune-telling book and then the other objects from her own pack, and carefully placed them onto the polished surface of the table. Lord Ravenglass took out a blue monocle, and peered through it at the items for a few moments.

"There's no doubt," he said, looking up, pleased. "All from the same world. And three at once. I think we may have found something I've been looking for rather a long time."

He smiled, and popped another pastry in his mouth.

"Congratulations, my dears," he said, smiling, and patting at the crumbs on his lips with his lace handkerchief. "You have made me very happy."

Dora was taken aback. From what the Druid and Caractacus had said, the objects were a cause for worry, not celebration. Why was Lord Ravenglass so pleased? And was he actually going to do anything to help? She didn't want to say anything that might annoy him, but she felt she had to at least ask.

"I'm sorry, your Lordship," she said, hesitantly.

"But the Druid said they had come from another world. All from the same one. Isn't that… dangerous?"

Lord Ravenglass laughed. "Oh, it's dangerous, all right. Thoroughly dangerous." He seemed to relish the idea. "But also very useful. There's only one thing that could have caused a rift serious enough to send three objects through from the same place. This is my best chance to find it in *years*… With a bit of luck, my agents are already there."

Dora was not reassured. She looked across at Jem, but he just seemed to be excited about the other worlds.

"So people *can* go there?" he asked, looking eager.

Lord Ravenglass eyed him speculatively.

"It's not very usual. But it can be done, when the need arises. Why – would you like to go?"

Dora felt her heart sink. She could tell from his expression that all Jem was concerned about was being sent to the world where the shiny red fortune-telling book belonged. And unfortunately, from the way Lord Ravenglass was looking at them both, it seemed likely Jem was going to get exactly what he wanted.

"It's true that children can often go where adults may not," he mused, stroking his chin. "And the more people looking for it, the better. You could take the objects back with you, too – might help calm the energies a little."

He clapped his hands.

"We'll try it, why not?" he said. "We can use one of the objects to create a portal, which will take you to that world. More importantly, it will take you back to where it came from, which means you will be *very* close to what's causing the rift."

His tone was matter-of-fact, but Dora noticed a kind of hunger in his expression as he went on. "There is a particular object… a jewel. It's almost certainly causing this situation. I need it. Well, that's to say, *the kingdom* needs it. It is extremely magical. It was lost from here many years ago, and I… *we*… need it back."

"What does it look like?" said Jem.

"It is a deep amber stone, orange-yellow, with dark flecks. Set in a bronze clasp."

Dora and Jem exchanged glances. Deep amber! This must be what Caractacus had been talking about. Lord Ravenglass obviously wanted it, and he wasn't going to do anything about the rift until he had it.

"We can find it for you, I'm sure! We'd be happy to go," Jem said firmly.

Dora frowned. She wasn't at all happy about it, in fact, but Jem was clearly determined to go, and if he went on his own, anything might happen to him. She nodded reluctantly.

"Well then, my dear Jem," said Lord Ravenglass, sitting back and popping another sweet into his mouth. "And my dear Dora. Let's get you there at once. After all, the sooner the better, eh?" He winked and laughed, and Dora swallowed. She couldn't get rid of a feeling that what they were about to do was very, very stupid.

A servant took Dora and Jem to clean the grime off their faces and get them fresh clothes. Then he whisked them off to see the queen.

The royal chambers, which were nearby, were rather dim and stuffy. The old, white-haired queen was sat very upright in a chair by the window, dressed in dark velvet. Around her neck was an intricate silver chain, and from it hung a bright glowing orange jewel in a silver clasp.

"The kingdom's remaining piece of deep amber," murmured Lord Ravenglass, nodding to the jewel. "The one you are looking for will be identical – I thought you'd better at least see what you are searching for."

He turned to the queen with a low bow.

"These are two of your loyal subjects, your Grace," he said loudly, as he ushered Dora and Jem forward. "They are going on an *important mission*, for m— For the kingdom. They seek your *blessing*."

The queen was very wrinkled and old. She smiled vaguely down at Dora.

"Ah, yes," she said. "Of course. I'll have the chocolate one, please."

"No – not pudding – *blessing*," bawled Lord Ravenglass. "I'm sending them to another *world*."

The queen turned to Lord Ravenglass and fixed him with a very hard stare from her blue eyes.

"Toads?" she said sternly. "What's all this nonsense about toads?"

Lord Ravenglass gritted his teeth. "No, Ma'am, nothing to do with toads," he bellowed.

"Another *world*. Dora and Jem – oh, never mind…
I'll sort it out myself. We will just take our leave,
your Grace. Need to be off soon." He bowed, with
a flourish, and the queen nodded regally.

"Very well," she said. "If you're sure. But
I wouldn't worry. You don't seem overweight to
me. Just nicely chubby."

Lord Ravenglass rolled his eyes, and they
followed him out of the room, and along the
corridor to his own chambers. Once they were
there, he turned, and smiled, showing altogether
too many teeth, Dora thought.

"Bit batty," he explained, unnecessarily. "No
need to worry – she's quite happy to leave things
to me most of the time." He ushered them further
into the chamber.

"Now, once you've got the amber, you come
straight back here," he said briskly. "And *when*
you get it," he put his face very close to theirs
and grinned, "I'll make you both knights of the
realm."

"But girls can't—" began Dora.

"I'm the king!" Lord Ravenglass interrupted,
with a wave of his white hand. "Well… that's to
say," he added swiftly, "I'm the heir – so I *will* be

the king. I can make *anyone* a knight of the realm! But I'll square it with the queen first, of course."

Jem looked at Dora, his eyes shining. But Dora was worried. She still wasn't really sure they were doing the right thing.

Lord Ravenglass closed the door of his chamber carefully, then rapidly showed Dora the magic necessary to get to another world and back again.

"You need an object from the other world to make the portal spell." He held out the goggles, demonstrated a complicated set of hand movements over them, and intoned a number of words. A wall of mist appeared, which he then dismissed with a gesture of his hand.

"Now you try," he said.

Dora took a deep breath, and tried to focus on the spell he had produced. After a few tries, she finally caught onto the particular twist in magic that was necessary. She closed her eyes, feeling for the cold strangeness of the goggles and then the warm, magic feel of her own world, and then used the words to create a link between them, with a kind of corkscrew magic that made her slightly dizzy.

When she opened her eyes, there was a white swirling mist in front of her, and Lord Ravenglass was looking pleased.

"You do the same to get back, only you'll need an object from the kingdom," he said, and handed them a small silver cup. "It's from my chambers – it will bring you straight back here. Off you go then – through the portal. Best of luck!"

He gave a regal wave of his jewelled hand.

Dora glanced at Jem. He was looking eager and slightly sick at the same time. He gave her a wry grin, and then they both took a deep breath and stepped into the mist.

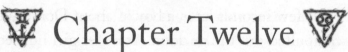# Chapter Twelve

Dora and Jem stepped out onto a smooth grey road surrounded by tall buildings. Behind them, the mist simply popped out of existence. The whole place smelt odd, and there was a dull, flat, absence of magic, none of the spicy warmth of spells that surrounded everything at home. Dora looked at the tall, well-built houses, a little like the houses in the city but flatter and larger and less jumbled together any old how. At least the sky looked the same, thought Dora, looking up with relief. And there seemed to be trees, and grass, and bushes.

"Right," Jem said. "Time to explore. Where do you think we should start?"

Dora was just about to say that they should start with the house directly in front of them, since that was where the portal had brought them. But before she could open her mouth, the door of the house burst open with a tremendous bang, and a white horse charged through it, up the garden and straight off down the road, carrying an oddly familiar figure in armour.

A few seconds later, a boy of about Dora's age catapulted out of the door. An older girl hurtled after him, throwing him a cloak of some kind. She had – Dora's eyes widened – *short* hair, and was wearing some kind of multi-coloured leggings. She was also holding a small box to her ear and talking into it as she ran. The boy charged after the galloping horse, followed closely by the girl.

Dora turned to Jem, her eyebrows raised.

"Am I dreaming, or was that Sir Bedwyr?"

Jem was grinning hugely. "I think our job here just got a whole lot more interesting!" he said, his face alight with excitement. "Come on Dora – after that horse!"

Simon was leaning against the plate-glass window of Simpson's Jewellers, panting hard. He had run all the way to the town centre, mostly managing to keep Sir Bedwyr in sight. The knight was just trotting gently along and stopping occasionally to ask passers-by where he might find a dragon.

Luckily, most of the people Sir Bedwyr had talked to had seemed to think he was part of a charity stunt, and had just laughed. But as he got closer to the town centre the roads got more crowded, and Sir Bedwyr, increasingly irritated by the cars he saw, had started turning off down a series of side-roads and pedestrianised alleyways. For a while, Simon had been able to follow the crashes and yells and commotion caused by the knight's progress, but now he'd completely lost the trail, and wasn't absolutely sure where Sir Bedwyr was. He also appeared to have a dead battery in his mobile, so he didn't know what had happened to Cat, or whether she'd managed to get hold of Albert Jemmet.

As he got his breath back, Simon became aware of a slight coldness at the back of his neck that made him feel as if he were being watched. He looked up and down the street, and then across to the other side, but there were just a few shoppers wandering past, and some children arguing loudly. Then the door of the jeweller's shop opened with an old-fashioned tinkle, and a dark figure emerged. As Simon turned his head, another dark figure seemed to materialise behind him.

"Good afternoon," said Mr Jones, with a smile that didn't reach his eyes, and he put his long white hand on Simon's shoulder.

Simon felt as if his feet had been superglued to the pavement. He tried to speak but his mouth wouldn't work. The cold hand of Mr Jones was biting into his shoulder, and it seemed as if ice crystals were forming in his blood, spreading down his arm and across the rest of his body.

"We'd just like a quiet word, if you don't mind, young man," said Mr Smith smoothly, moving closer to where Simon was standing and reaching out his hand to grip Simon's other shoulder. "Lord Ravenglass is starting to get a little bit impatient…" His fingers were only a few centimetres away when there was a piercing scream and a huge clattering. Simon felt himself wrenched away from the two men just a split second before Smith and Jones were bowled over by a great white horse galloping down the street.

"Quick! Down here!" came a voice, and Simon was hustled down a narrow passage between the jewellers and a card shop by a rather short, stout figure in blue overalls.

"Albert!" he said as they hurried down the passageway and took a swift left around the back of WHSmith. "Thanks! How did you know…?"

"I didn't," said Albert Jemmet shortly, stopping behind a large wheelie bin. He dusted Simon down, looking like he was checking him over for damage. "You're lucky – I was following the knight when I saw you and pulled you out of the way. Bit of a close shave, that."

"Where's Cat?" said Simon. "Did she call you?"

Jemmet nodded. "She's gone round the other way to the square, trying to head him off. Come on – we'd better get going, before Smith and Jones pick themselves up off the road, or that nuisance on the horse causes any more damage. The last thing we need is him getting himself locked up where I can't get at him."

A large swathe had been cut through the market in Wemworthy town centre. It was as if a dinosaur had come to life and trampled its way across the neat rows of stalls. Splintered bits of wood, pulped fruit and vegetables, brightly coloured T-shirts and various bits of plastic lay trampled on the ground, while small knots of people were gathering, looking shell-shocked. Some of them were attempting to clear up the mess, but most just stood there, clearly amazed and relieved that they had survived the carnage. A number of cars were slewn across the road, some with smashed windows, and most with doors left open after their drivers had escaped.

The police constable on duty was feeling rather appalled. Normally, his morning shift in Wemworthy town centre was calm and uneventful. Even on a market day, like this one, he usually just spent his time finding the odd lost toddler or exchanging a few stern words with a stall-holder whose van was blocking a side street. But today he had been stopped at least five times by members of the public wittering on about a knight in armour, and now he'd reached the market square it looked as if someone had chosen his shift to re-enact the Battle of Bosworth.

"Oh, Constable, thank goodness!" said a woman stall-holder as she spotted the policeman. "There's a madman on the loose! He's dressed as a knight – on a horse – just smashed his way across the market saying he'd come to save us!"

"Called us peasants!" added another woman with great indignation. "Said 'I've come to save you, peasants!' and then knocked all the toy rabbits off my stall with his stupid great horse!"

Everyone, now that they'd spotted the policeman, started to rush over to give their version of events. A tall well-dressed man who appeared to be the owner of a smashed BMW tried to push to the front of the crowd.

"Ruddy maniac!" he spluttered. "Some kind of anti-roads protestor. Stuck his sword right through my windscreen! Look at it! Said he was protecting the peasants from my *dark magic...* What kind of ruddy Harry Potter nonsense is that?"

"Look at my stall!" shouted another angry member of the crowd. "He rode right through it!"

"He smashed all my hand-thrown pottery fruit bowls," wailed another.

"Look at my car! The horse kicked my bonnet in!"

"You've got to *do* something!"

Police Constable Taylor felt as if he'd walked

into a bad dream. In fact, he seriously thought about closing his eyes and hoping it would all have gone away when he opened them again. But before he could try it, the noise of the crowd raised itself a pitch and several people shouted at once, "There he is! That's him! Arrest him!"

Trotting down the road was a knight in shining armour on a white horse, with a sword in his hand.

Constable Taylor blinked.

The knight was still there.

He had dark curly hair and blue eyes, and as he reached the policeman he halted, and held his sword up in a salute.

"Good sir, I have rid this market of the metallic beasts that had it surrounded, and have set free these good peasants you see before you. I await your thanks."

Constable Taylor realised that he was staring at the knight with his mouth open. He closed it quickly, and cleared his throat, trying to summon up a Voice of Authority. It was distinctly difficult when the person you were trying to impress was at least six feet higher up than you and was holding a sword dangerously close to your head, but Constable Taylor did his best.

"I am afraid I must request that you accompany me to the police station, sir. You are under arrest for disturbance of the peace and various counts of damage to property. You do not have to say anything—"

But he got no further, because the knight simply frowned, and leaned forward, and pointed his sword at Constable Taylor's chest.

"Sir, your thanks are a little hard to understand, but no matter. I am afraid I cannot join you at your station, tempting though I am sure your feast would be. I have a Quest to fulfil. Can you direct me to a dragon, or perhaps the sorcerer who set these metal beasts on your peasants?"

Constable Taylor was embarrassed to find that his mouth was open again. He shut it firmly, and went for his radio. But the knight was already wheeling his horse around.

"Farewell, peasants," he called. "Since none of you can help me, I shall try my luck westwards. I did think that I heard a roar from that direction that had the very tone of a dragon... Till we meet again!"

He waved his sword to them all, and clattered

off down the road, just as two children burst through the crowd and shouted something that sounded like, "Sir Bedwyr! Come back!"

Constable Taylor shook his head, and spoke into his radio.

"This is PC Taylor, requesting back-up. Serious incident Wemworthy town centre. Four cars requested. Repeat, *four* cars requested. Suspect heading down the High Street towards Whites Lane."

Chapter Thirteen

Sir Bedwyr made his last stand outside the Green Dragon Inn, on the outskirts of Wemworthy. Luckily for the police back-up he had dismounted from his horse and left him outside while he went to ask for directions to the dragon. When the knight came out, Dappletoes was in custody and there were four police cars surrounding the door to the inn.

"YOU ARE UNDER ARREST FOR BREACH OF THE PEACE AND SERIOUS AFFRAY," called a policeman through a loudhailer, standing well back behind one of the cars. The other officers closed in slowly, keeping a careful eye on Sir Bedwyr's sword hand. Behind him, the heavy oak door of the inn banged shut.

Sir Bedwyr drew himself up to his full

height and laughed contemptuously.

"Miscreant peasants! I am a knight of Roland Castle. Out of my way, or I shall chop your livers into small pieces for the rooks to feast on!"

The police officers looked at each other nervously, but stood their ground. Sir Bedwyr unsheathed his sword and there was a tense stand-off.

"Now, now, sir," said Constable Taylor, who was directly in front of the knight. "There's no need for any fighting. We'd just like you to put down the sword and come with us."

"I shall give you to a count of five to retreat," said Sir Bedwyr angrily. "Then I shall consider any remaining men my enemies and fell them instantly!"

Constable Taylor looked at his back-up helplessly. There wasn't anything in the police manual about dealing with knights and swords. It was all rather difficult. He really wished he'd stayed in bed that morning with a headache.

"ONE!" roared Sir Bedwyr.

"Umm – shall we call for more help?" hissed the policeman closest to Constable Taylor with a worried frown.

"TWO!"

Constable Taylor rubbed his chin thoughtfully. He was wondering whether to order a strategic retreat when a young girl ran out of the crowd and pushed her way through the circle of policemen.

"Sir Bedwyr!" she shouted. "It's me – Dora! Put your sword down!"

The knight frowned, and stopped counting, but he didn't lower his sword.

"What in the name of magic are you doing here, Dora?' he hissed. "Out of the way! I'm quelling the local peasantry!"

"No, no, you mustn't!" said Dora, desperately. "They'll lock you up!"

As Sir Bedwyr hesitated, Jem wriggled his way through the police circle as well, and ran up to join Dora.

"Jem!" said Sir Bedwyr with a look of disgust. "How do you always manage to turn up when there's trouble?"

Simon, standing at the edge of the small crowd that had gathered near the Green Dragon, wondered where the two newcomers had appeared from. Had they come out of the cellar as well? They were both dressed in slightly odd, old-fashioned clothes, and there was something different about the way they moved and gestured. Simon watched in fascination as Sir Bedwyr, deep in consultation with the two children, failed to notice the inn door opening slowly and carefully behind him.

"Enough!" roared the knight after a few minutes. "Out of my way, you two. It's time the people of this strange land learned to show some respect to a knight of the realm. Three, Four, FIVE!"

But as he started forward to deal with the policemen, Sir Bedwyr was caught completely unawares by the landlord of the Green Dragon Inn, who emerged from the open door and landed a perfect blow on the back of the knight's head with a full bottle of Gordon's gin. Sir Bedwyr hit the ground like a felled tree and the small crowd that had gathered cheered and clapped.

As the policemen approached with handcuffs, Albert Jemmet pushed his way past Simon and went to have a brief word with the two children standing helplessly next to the knight. Together, they seemed to be trying to argue with the arresting officer, but Simon couldn't catch much except the odd word or phrases.

"Yes, their uncle... if we could just... should have taken his medicine... very sorry... No, we really..."

But the policeman was clearly adamant. Sir Bedwyr was going down to the station to be processed. He took Albert Jemmet's phone number and promised to call him, and then they drove off smartly, after requesting that the crowd disperse and go home.

"Well," said Albert, as he came over to where Simon had just been joined by a breathless Cat. "We've got a pretty situation here, I must say. Simon, Cat – this is Dora, and this here is Jem. They're from the same place as the knight."

The four children looked at each other. Dora started to curtsey, and then stopped, feeling confused. Did they even do that in this world? Judging from the look on Cat's face, she guessed not. Jem stepped forward, and gave them both a flamboyant bow.

"Well met!" he said. "Looks like we've all been chasing after Sir Bedwyr. Most eligible knight in Roland Castle, but not exactly the brightest..."

He grinned at Cat, who was still breathing hard, having run all the way to the Green Dragon.

She nodded back. He looked friendly enough, she thought, and the girl with dark plaits looked rather sweet, if a bit shy. Both of them, though, had a strange way of standing, an odd air about them – as if they didn't quite belong.

Simon nodded at Dora, and then Jem. "Welcome to… er… our world," he said, and immediately felt ridiculous, but Dora gave him a warm smile, and nodded back.

"Well then," said Albert, taking charge. "Introductions over. Maybe we'd better all go back to Simon and Cat's place for a nice cup of tea. I think we need to talk."

Albert stirred six sugars into his tea and then, after a pause, added another two.

"Helps me think," he said, as Cat raised her eyebrows.

They were all seated round the kitchen table with a hot mug of tea and a plate of chocolate biscuits. Jem and Dora had looked rather suspiciously at the biscuits to start with, but Jem was now happily tucking into his fifth.

"Right," said Albert, as he took a great gulp of his sweet tea. "Let's get this straight." He pointed his teaspoon at Dora. "Lord Ravenglass sent you and this young man through a portal from the palace? With the missing items from this world?"

"Yes," said Dora, and she tipped up the pack, sending the goggles and the peculiar boxes tumbling out.

"That's my camera!" said Cat, and seized it. "How did *you* end up with it?"

"And my DS," said Simon, picking up the console wonderingly. He turned to Cat. "And I *told* you I didn't have anything to do with your missing camera!"

She made a face at him, and went on checking the camera over. After a few moments, she looked up with a bemused expression. "What's with all these pictures of noses and warts? And is that a knight falling off his horse?"

Jem grinned. "Sir Rodrick," he explained. "He gave me a good hiding for that one. But what about the fortune-telling machine?" he added, eagerly, pointing to the DS. "How does it really work?"

"It plays games," said Simon, opening it. "The one in there at the moment is called *Castle Quest*. You choose a character, then you have to go through various levels and collect gold coins and stuff."

He turned it on, and demonstrated. Cat watched the two boys, heads together, bent over the DS. Jem was exclaiming in amazement at how quickly Simon was able to battle with evil dwarves and collect gold coins, Simon was equally impressed at how far Jem had got with no previous experience. She turned to Dora. "Boys, eh?" she said, one eyebrow raised. Dora looked rather startled, and smiled tentatively.

Albert Jemmet tapped the top of the table with his teaspoon.

"All right, enough of that," he said sternly to the two boys. "We've got a serious situation on our hands here. Things have been slipping back and forth between the two worlds for a few days now – Cat's camera, the DS, the sword. That's not normal at all. We've clearly got a very large rift that's getting worse by the minute – and now it's big enough to drag across a whole horse and an associated idiot in armour. If Jem and Dora are right, then Lord Ravenglass knows all about it, but there's still no sign of it being shut down by anyone in the kingdom."

He tapped the display on one of his strange electrical machines, where the needle was quivering madly back and forth.

"Energies all over the place. If the rift doesn't get shut down soon, the worlds are going to start bleeding into each other."

"What do you mean, bleeding into each other?" said Cat. "Is that dangerous?"

Albert frowned. "Very dangerous. Which means we need to start working together to find what's causing it."

"You said there was a rift," put in Jem. "Caractacus said the same, and that it needed to be shut down. But how do you know about the rift, and the kingdom? Where do you come into all this?"

Albert looked at them all sternly.

"I come into this because I'm *from* the kingdom. And as it happens, it was Caractacus who contacted me about the rift in the first place. I'm an agent for the Great Forest, and it's my job to keep this particular world safe and balanced. And I must say, there are some people who've been making my job damn near impossible." He pointed his spoon at Simon. "You've got a whiff of magic about you. You *and* Cat. And you know something you're not saying."

Albert leaned back in his chair, and fixed them all in turn with his shrewd gaze. "We need to focus," he said. "There's deep amber at the bottom of this, or my name's not Albert Jemmet. We need to find it quick, and close it down."

Dora and Jem exchanged glances. Deep amber! It was what they were supposed to be looking for. Simon opened his mouth to say something, but at that moment Albert's mobile went off with a loud electronic fanfare, and he whipped it out of his overall pocket, disappearing into the hall to answer it.

When he returned a few minutes later, he looked grim. "Damn and blast! That's the police. That brainless fool of a knight has escaped from police custody. I need to get after him. And while I'm gone *you*," he pointed at them all, as he grabbed his canvas bag and made for the door, "need to start working together. You need to find me that piece of deep amber, before we're all in a very great deal of trouble indeed."

Chapter Fourteen

The front door shut with a determined bang, and the four children were left sitting at the kitchen table in silence. No one was quite sure what to say. Cat was stunned by the idea that Albert thought she had magic. Simon, who'd always secretly hoped that he might have, was thrilled that it was actually true. But then he started thinking about the box, and wondering whether they should show it to Dora and Jem. Dora was still considering what Albert had said about the amber needing to be shut down, and worrying whether Lord Ravenglass was altogether trustworthy. And Jem was just thinking about his chances of being made a knight.

After a while, Cat made an effort to pull herself together and take charge. She turned to Jem.

"So, if you came here from… that other world,"
she said, "does that mean you can do magic?"

He shook his head. "No – not a spark of it,"
he said and jerked his thumb at Dora. "Dora's the
one with the magic."

Simon looked interested. "Are you?" he said.
"Could you teach us?"

Dora glanced over at him. Albert was right,
there was a feel of magic about Simon, bubbling
under the surface.

"Maybe," she said cautiously. "This world is
a bit odd – there doesn't really seem to be much
magic here at all. But there's definitely some
here in this house. Have you got anything odd
upstairs?" She was sure there was a buzz of magic
coming from above her head – a buzz of rather
agitated magic, at that.

Simon and Cat exchanged glances, then Cat
nodded.

"Albert's right. We're going to have to work
together… The thing is, we've got a box upstairs
and we think it might have this deep amber in it
that Albert was talking about. But we can't open
it. Simon – go and get it, and bring it down."

Simon jumped up and left the kitchen.

When he returned, he was carrying the wooden box in his hands, and he put it carefully in the middle of the table. As he did so, Dora was sure she heard a rather faraway voice saying crossly, "Oh, will you just get on with it!"

She looked at Jem, who had a faint grin on his face, and she felt the corner of her mouth twitch.

"You've got a ghost in there," she said. "And it sounds a bit cross."

"A ghost?" said Simon, looking alarmed "Really – a ghost?" He looked at Cat. "Do you think…?"

She gulped, and nodded.

He turned to Dora. "It's Great-Aunt Irene's box. And – the voice sounds very like her. I don't know how she could possibly be in there but…"

"It'll be her for sure," said Jem. "Why haven't you let her out? Great-aunts don't usually like to be kept waiting. You need to get that box open."

"We've been trying!" said Cat indignantly. "Nothing's worked so far. I think I know what the symbols mean, but we couldn't get it to open."

Dora peered at the carved symbols. Three of them were clearly the instructions for a powerful opening spell. The fourth was a painted amber jewel. She glanced across at Jem, who nodded. This must be the amber Lord Ravenglass was after. The question was, should they open it? Should they just take it straight back to Lord Ravenglass, or should they find out more about what was going on? As Dora hesitated, an imperious voice rose from the box.

"In the name of the kingdom and the Great Forest, I demand that this box be opened RIGHT NOW!"

Dora jumped. She instinctively raised her hands and said the words of the opening spell. The box burst into flames, then instantly cooled, so that frost started crackling along the edges of the carvings, and then the lid flew open, releasing what felt like a tornado.

Cat and Simon looked at each other, wide-eyed. As the wind whipped their hair round their faces and hurled random bits of newspaper across the kitchen, a stream of silvery dust shot up to the ceiling and then gently settled back down into a human shape, like fine sand filling a glass container. Finally they could see, standing on the kitchen table, the rather gaunt figure of an old lady with silver hair and a cane looking down at them disapprovingly. Cat realised she had her mouth open, and shut it rapidly. Next to her, Simon was looking equally taken aback, but Jem and Dora seemed to think this was all quite normal.

"Out at last!" said the silvery lady, with a sigh. "It was getting very uncomfortable indeed in that wretched box!"

She bent down and clambered ungracefully off the table and then turned to survey them all.

"Well now," she said. "Catrin and Simon. How nice. I thought it must be you, all that incompetence with the brandy. Thank goodness you seem to have found yourselves a friend who knows how to *use* magic."

She gave them all a piercing look from her pale silvery eyes and rapped the table with her cane. Simon was startled to find that it made a very solid-sounding noise. In fact, Great-Aunt Irene was starting to look very solid all round, turning rapidly from a silvery wraith to a perfectly normal if somewhat unimpressed old lady. Although, he noted, it was still just possible to see the outline of the back door though her head.

"Well?' she said, expectantly. "Where is my

good-for-nothing son? Why on earth is there just a rabble of children here?"

"Your son?" said Cat. "Do you mean Uncle Lou?"

"Yes, of course. Louis," said Great-Aunt Irene, looking, if possible, even more disapproving. "I thought he'd be here by now. Avoiding trouble, as usual, I see."

"I'm not sure where he is," said Cat. "Mum said he left years ago."

"He did indeed," sniffed Great-Aunt Irene. "He had a disagreement with your mother. I rather think she said she never wanted to see him again. Most awkward. So he disappeared off travelling, and it's been very difficult to get hold of him ever since. But he really ought to be back by now. He's meant to have the amber, as he very well knows."

Simon, who had been unable to take his eyes off Great-Aunt Irene since she had appeared in front of him, suddenly remembered what else was supposed to have been in the box. He turned, to see Jem carefully lifting up an amber jewel, with an elaborate bronze clasp and length of chain attached. Cat, following his gaze, saw the amber and gasped.

The clasp was in the shape of two intertwining branches, with tiny bronze-coloured leaves, winding around the central jewel. Glowing through the bronze like a miniature sun was a deep orange-yellow stone, with darker flecks and whorls inside it that looked as if they were continuously moving. It was almost as if there was a fire deep inside the stone. In fact, Jem was blowing on his fingers as if he had scorched them, and was now very carefully holding it only by the clasp. He met Simon's eyes, and gave a wry grin.

"Looks like this is the deep amber, then," he said. "It's a bit hot."

"Of course it's hot, foolish boy!" said Great-Aunt Irene. "It was activated days ago. Random magical activity from young Simon here – sleeping almost right above it. It's been getting more and more unstable ever since. It was not much fun being locked in a box right on top of it, I can tell you!"

Dora looked at the amber jewel swinging from Jem's hand. She could feel that it had immensely strong power, but there was also a crackling, sparking, uncontrolled magic that surrounded the amber like a halo. It felt distinctly dangerous.

"Um, sorry, Aunt Irene," said Cat. "But how exactly did you end up in the box with it? And how did it get activated? And what can we do to shut it down?"

Great-Aunt Irene nodded in approval. "All very sensible questions," she said. "Maybe I'd better explain."

She raised one eyebrow at Simon, who looked blank until she impatiently indicated a chair with her cane. Hurriedly he pulled it out, and she settled herself on it with a creaking sigh.

"Well," she said. "First things first. The amber belongs to me, or it did while I was alive. Deep amber is always the property of an heir to the kingdom, and my family is originally from that world. When I died, it was supposed to go to my son." She sniffed. "If there's no heir to take it immediately, the most recent holder is bound to the amber as a ghost until it can be passed on to the new heir. I didn't realise that meant literally stuck in the box with it until I came to, a few days after passing away, and found myself under the floorboards."

Great-Aunt Irene shook her head crossly. "Anyway, I had arranged for a message to be sent to Louis if I died, so I just settled down to wait for him. And then Simon accidentally activated the amber with his magic and opened a rift to the kingdom. No doubt all sorts of nonsense has got pulled from one side to the other by now." She raised her eyebrows at them, and they all nodded. "I can't think why Queen Igraine hasn't used the kingdom's amber to close the rift from her side."

"Well, we were sent to tell the palace," said Dora. "The Druid thought they would sort it out. But the queen is a bit old, and Lord Ravenglass..." she trailed off, not sure how much to say.

"Ravenglass?" said Great-Aunt Irene sharply. "Is he in charge now? I never did trust that boy." She gave Dora and Jem a hard stare. "He's after *this* amber, isn't he? That's why they haven't shut the rift down yet. He'll be wanting to find out where the amber is, first. I imagine he asked you two to bring it back to him."

"No he didn't," said Jem with an innocent expression. "He never said anything about that. He just said to take the goggles and stuff back."

"Hmm," was all Great-Aunt Irene said, but she still managed to make it sound as if judge, jury and court had all found Jem guilty of appalling lying and sentenced him to life as a worm.

Simon had felt a slight shiver down his back as the name Ravenglass was mentioned. Where had he heard that name before? It made him feel cold, and on the edge of something dark... Did it have anything to do with Smith and Jones? But as he grasped for the memory, Cat's phone went off, and she flapped at everyone to keep quiet while she answered it.

It was Albert. After a few minutes, she finished the call and looked up.

"He's found Sir Bedwyr. He's broken into Sunset Court – the old people's home. Albert says can we come and help. And we should bring the sword."

Chapter Fifteen

Sunset Court Home for the Elderly was a Victorian manor house on the outskirts of town. It had been built by a man who had made a fortune selling rubber boots, and had wanted to live like a lord, so it had turrets and a large ornamental moat.

When Sir Bedwyr had spotted it, it had been clear to him that here, at last, was a proper castle. His Quest must be to defend it from all attackers – especially those strangely hostile knights in their blue uniforms who had captured him earlier. Luckily for him, the first person he met as he marched across the lawn towards the main entrance was an imperious old lady in a wheelchair, who insisted he bowed and kissed her hand.

"I am Queen Elizabeth the First," she said.

"I accept your fealty, good sir knight. Please join my retinue." She had waved her hand graciously at a rather upright and well-built old man with a white handlebar moustache.

"Sorry about that," said the man with a grin. "We humour her, you know. Are you with a theatre troop or something? Pleased to meet you, anyway – I'm Colonel Alfred Fairfax, formerly of the Guards."

"And I am Sir Bedwyr, of Roland Castle," said Sir Bedwyr, bowing. "I am here to help you defend the castle against your enemies. Or maybe a dragon. But probably your enemies. They may not be far behind me."

"Dragon, eh?" said Colonel Fairfax, twirling his moustache. "That sounds fun. One of these drama groups where everyone has to get involved, is that it? Brightening up the life of the dull old folks' home?" He rubbed his hands. "Well, I'm all for that. Bit of excitement. War games, that sort of thing. I'm always telling them we need a bit more going on out here. What would you like me to do?"

Sir Bedwyr eyed the Colonel in approval. He was clearly another military man. Between the two of them, they should get the castle set up for defence in no time.

He and Colonel Fairfax rapidly spread the word about the imminent siege of the castle, helped by Queen Elizabeth the First calling all her loyal subjects to arms. Most of the residents were under the impression that this was some elaborate game, but a few were half inclined to believe that it really was a siege, and they were being called on to defend queen and country. Whatever the truth, there was a huge level of enthusiasm for the preparations, and the Colonel started directing several residents to build a barricade across the driveway.

It was Vincent Trimbleby, however, who'd been an intelligence officer in the Second World War, who came up with the master stroke. He had grasped that the castle was about to be attacked by the police, and that they had to prevent them from taking anyone alive. He immediately set to and cut the telephone wires, and then he locked the entire management team in their meeting room on the second floor.

"In league with the authorities," he explained, tapping one finger on his nose meaningfully.

"Would have betrayed us all, no question. What can you expect of people who shove nasty pills down your throat and make you take a bath every day?"

Norah Jones, eighty-four, took the key from him and dropped it down the front of her dress with a wink. She hadn't had so much fun since the day a whole group of them had escaped during a fire drill. They had spent several hours at the local fun fair before they'd been rounded up and returned to the home in disgrace. She rather thought they'd get in even more trouble this time, but she didn't really care. As she said to her friend, Ermintrude, Sir Bedwyr might be as mad as a bag of frogs, but he had lovely eyes. And it was a lot more exciting preparing for battle than for hot milk and biscuits before bed.

Cat explained the plan as they set off down the road to the bus stop. Albert would use the sword to open a portal back to Roland Castle. Then Sir Bedwyr just had to be rounded up and persuaded to charge through it with his horse and that was that. End of problem, according to Albert. Although there was still the amber to worry about, and the rift to shut down – but first things first, he'd said.

Great-Aunt Irene had insisted on coming with them, which meant the box with the amber had had to come too, since she was still magically bound to it. Cat had the box in her rucksack. As soon as she'd seen the amber, Cat had had a strong desire to hold it. But she was wary of getting scorched fingers like Jem, and after he'd reluctantly put the jewel back, she had just carefully shut the box and stuffed it in her rucksack without touching the amber at all.

Simon, meanwhile, had wrapped the sword in a bath towel, and then put it in a black bin liner. It wasn't very dignified, keeping it in a bin bag, he thought, but he still felt absurdly happy carrying it. He could feel the faint buzz of magic from it, even through the towel, and it gave his arm a tingling feeling of excitement.

He glanced over at Cat. They hadn't really had a chance to talk, what with the others milling around, and the need to get to Albert as quickly as possible. He wondered if she was feeling the same mixture of confusion and excitement as he was. The ghost of Great-Aunt Irene – what was *that* about? Part of him felt as if he was just in a dream. And yet there was another part of him that felt as if it was everything *else* that had been a dream – their life before the sword appeared. This tingle of magic in his arm, and the talk of other worlds, rifts, deep amber and knights – he was sure it was all connected to his dad, and right now it felt more real and important than anything Simon could remember.

They made an odd assortment, marching down the road to the bus stop – Jem and Dora in their odd clothes, Simon with his bin bag, and Cat anxiously turning around at regular intervals to make sure the now almost invisible Great-Aunt Irene was still floating along behind them. The bus driver looked a little suspiciously at Simon's package, but he let them on, and it wasn't long before they had been deposited on the outskirts of town, a few minutes' walk from the main entrance to Sunset Court.

As the bus roared off, the nearby undergrowth rustled, and Albert emerged from behind a large tree.

"Excellent!" he said. "All of you. Hopefully we can get everyone sent off home together.

And – my sainted eyebrows! Is that your great-aunt you've got with you?!"

There was a whisper of wind, as the ghost of Great-Aunt Irene swooped rapidly behind Cat and gave an embarrassed cough.

"Albert!" she said, in a rather mortified tone. "I hoped you wouldn't notice. I'm not really fit to be seen. I'm extremely... transparent. Most regrettably, I seem to be stuck here with the amber until we can find a way to pass it on."

Albert grinned and bowed in Great-Aunt Irene's general direction. "Well, I have to say, I'm not altogether surprised. I always thought you might be an heir. And when all those objects started going back and forth in the house, it seemed pretty clear there was amber there somewhere..." He stopped, and glanced quickly at Cat's rucksack. "So does that mean you've brought it along? The amber?"

She nodded.

He rubbed his chin, thoughtfully. "Might complicate matters. But I suppose you couldn't just leave it there." He glanced across at Great-Aunt Irene. "If you wouldn't mind just getting back in the box with it for the moment," he said, rather apologetically, "it might be safer all round."

She drew herself up, haughtily, looking as if she were going to object, but then reluctantly nodded. "As you say, Albert. It might be safest." She shimmered, then a stream of silvery dust flowed into Cat's rucksack and she was gone.

"Right," said Albert, looking round at them all. "First thing to do is get hold of that idiot and his horse."

Chapter Sixteen

It was several hours after Sir Bedwyr disappeared that the Druid got to hear about it. Sol the butcher's boy had seen him ride into a patch of nothingness, and had spent most of the day regaling the castle servants with the tale before he thought to tell the Druid.

"You saw him disappear?' said the Druid sternly. "And you didn't come and tell me about it *at once*?"

Sol looked petrified. He had once been discovered keeping pet frogs in one of the Druid's cauldrons, and had spent a week with pink hair and green skin as a punishment. To say nothing of having to scour clean every cauldron in the castle. Since then he'd avoided the Druid whenever possible.

"Um… sorry. I didn't think… I wasn't sure. It was from a distance."

"Where, and when?"

"This morning, I was out checking traps in the meadow. He was trotting back towards the castle and then he just… vanished. Winked out. I wasn't sure if it was magic, or if a bit of the sun got in my eyes."

The Druid held Sol's gaze for a few moments, and then sighed.

"Go away, idiot boy. But next time something like this happens, tell someone who might be able to do something about it, not your good-for-nothing friends."

Sol escaped rapidly and the Druid headed for his chambers, looking worried. As he opened the door, he spotted a blue caterpillar curled up asleep on his window ledge.

"Ah," said the caterpillar, waking up as the Druid strode over. "You're back. Good."

"Caractacus," said the Druid, looking taken aback. "What are you doing here?"

"Well, let's see," said the caterpillar, ticking each point off on one of his many legs. "There's the three objects, possibly more, that have fallen through to this side over the last few days. There's the sword. That went the other way around the same time. And then there's the rather large knight and horse that seem to have crossed over just this morning – causing no end of havoc, according to Albert. It all adds up to a piece of deep amber that needs dealing with, immediately."

The Druid threw himself into a large carved oak chair with an exasperated expression. "I know!" he said. "But I can't go back. I promised I wouldn't interfere. I did send Jem and Dora with a message for Ravenglass and the queen. And I made sure they went through the forest, so you'd know as well. Why hasn't someone dealt with it?"

"Well, Albert's doing his best," said Caractacus. "But Smith and Jones are involved. And Lord Ravenglass is up to something. The forest would like to send another agent."

He looked hard at the Druid.

"But I quit!" said the Druid. "Years ago."

"Hmm," said Caractacus. "And I retired. Not that you'd know it. They never stop sending me to sort things out."

The Druid held his head in his hands for a moment, and then stood up. It was no good.

He'd tried very hard not to get involved. He'd tried to keep his promise. But it seemed that no one was just going to get on and deal with that amber. The rift was getting bigger, and now it had dragged Sir Bedwyr across. The Druid sighed. Caractacus was right. He would just have to go himself.

He opened a small drawer in the cupboard opposite, and took out a small, carefully wrapped packet. He gently removed the wrapping. Nestling in the folds of fine parchment was a small, rectangular piece of orange and yellow card. On it were printed the words: CHEAP DAY RETURN, LONDON TO BASINGSTOKE. The Druid made a series of complicated hand manoeuvres over the card, said the words of the portal spell, then carefully stepped through the swirling white mist that appeared in his room, into the grey dusk of a deserted railway-station platform.

Sunset Court was prepared for battle. Colonel Fairfax had doled out garden forks and shovels and a number of particularly heavy brass lampstands to the eager troops. Sir Bedwyr had levered a long, straight piece of heating pipe off the wall with one of the shovels, and hefted it experimentally in his hand.

"Perfect," he said, handing it to Colonel Fairfax. "Just the weight and balance of a good broadsword."

Then the residents had constructed a number of booby traps, and settled down in the hall to wait for action.

It wasn't long in coming. Mrs Allsop, the matron, had not been at the management meeting on the second floor. She had been at the local garden centre, putting in an order for twelve tubs of geraniums to brighten up the patio. When she returned, she was extremely surprised to find a whole pile of the care home's furniture stacked in the middle of the driveway, preventing her Fiat Panda from getting further than halfway to the house. There also appeared to be a white horse wandering around the grounds.

She marched up to the front door, and opened it crossly, calling out for her deputy to come and see about the mess on the driveway, and the strange horse. But she wasn't more than two steps inside the door before a whole bucket of water tipped down on her head from the balcony above the entrance hallway, and a knight in armour approached her waving a very long sword.

"Wha- wha- what?" gasped Mrs Allsop, trying to wipe the water out of her eyes, and back away at the same time. "What on earth's going on?"

"We are under siege," said Sir Bedwyr. "Are you with us or against us?"

"Don't be ridiculous!" said the matron, sounding a good deal braver than she felt. She glanced past the knight at the massed residents of the home, with their shovels and forks and excited faces, and felt a twinge of doubt, but she tried not to let it show. "You must all stop this silly nonsense at once," she said firmly. "Or I shall call the police!"

Albert Jemmet had noted the matron's approach. He decided to let her go in first, and see what happened. Gesturing to the others to follow him, he crept up to the front door, where he could hear Sir Bedwyr and the matron arguing loudly. As he hesitated, a shrill voice from one of the windows above the entrance shouted, "There's more of them! Intruders – at the front door – quickly!"

Albert shoved open the door and marched in purposefully. "Now then, all!" he said firmly. "Time to stop this little game. Sir Bedwyr – we've come to take you back to the kingdom."

But his voice was lost in a general shout and crash as most of the residents hurled themselves down the long hallway, with Sir Bedwyr roaring over the top of them all, "Charge! For glory and freedom!"

Albert and the others all dived sideways through large open double doors, into what looked like the ballroom of the manor house, but now served as the residents' lounge. It was a long room with various sofas and armchairs dotted about, and a large Persian rug in the centre. Crashing after them through the double doors came several elderly warriors waving garden forks, a tall man with a white moustache wielding what looked like a large section of central-heating pipe, and a small but sprightly old lady waving an umbrella and shouting: "For England and your queen!" Behind them all charged Sir Bedwyr, waving his sword.

"Sir Bedwyr!" shouted Dora, as she dodged an old man with a shovel. "It's us! We're here to rescue you!"

Simon ducked behind an overstuffed armchair just as the man with the moustache brought the central-heating pipe crashing down exactly where his head had been a moment before. The chair sagged, but held firm, and the man raised the pipe for another go. Simon just managed to use the sword, still wrapped in its bin bag, to fend off the second blow.

Albert Jemmet was on the other side of the room, using a dining chair to keep off two residents with garden forks and Jem was pinned to the wall by the sprightly old lady, who was poking her umbrella into his middle. Dora had been chased behind a sofa. Luckily at that moment, Cat managed to throw herself at Sir Bedwyr's legs and rugby-tackle him to the ground, his sword flying out of his hand and halfway across the lounge. Albert Jemmet swept his chair sideways at his two assailants, and as they staggered into each other, he picked up the sword and waved it over his head.

"Enough!" he roared. "This stops NOW! We've come to get Sir Bedwyr and if we don't get him home very soon I wouldn't like to say what might happen."

Sir Bedwyr pulled himself up to his feet, slightly dazed. He gave Cat a hurt and betrayed look, and frowned at Simon. Then he pointed an accusing finger at Albert Jemmet.

"You!" he said. "You were at the dragon inn. What are you doing *here*? What's going on?"

"It's complicated," said Albert. "But first of all, can you please call off your troops?"

Sir Bedwyr looked like he was trying to work out some particularly tricky long division in his head. After a few moments, he nodded, and gestured to the residents. "Let them go. They're not part of the enemy forces."

The residents lowered their weapons, and took a few steps back. But then Colonel Fairfax gave a warning shout.

"Not so fast, everyone! We've got trouble!"

Standing in the open doorway were two tall thin figures in shiny black suits.

Mr Smith and Mr Jones.

 # Chapter Seventeen

Dora looked at the two men, with their pale skin and deep black eyes, and shivered. There was a kind of cold magic concentrated around them, a sense of age and deep malevolence. She had never felt anything so strong and frightening in all the kingdom.

"Albert Jemmet," said the younger of the two men, and gave a slight bow.

"Mr Smith," said Albert grimly. "And Mr Jones." Dora watched as he reached inside his canvas bag and brought out a peculiar contraption with a large rubber bulb attached to a trumpet-shaped mouthpiece. "I'd be getting along, if I were you. Vermin are not wanted here."

Dora could tell Albert was trying to sound confident, but it was clear he was anything but… and the two men knew it.

Mr Jones laughed – a sound like pebbles rattling together. "Oh no, Albert, that won't do," he said with a grin. "Won't do at all. There's no protection on *this* house. No shield runes built into the bricks. No enchantments on the doors and windows. Nothing to stop us bringing *all* our power in with us…"

As he spoke, he stretched his arms out wide, and called out, in a dry, rasping voice. Dora felt the cold, dark magic around both men grow stronger, seeming to solidify… Mr Smith added his voice to his companion's, and Dora flinched. Suddenly there was a great billowing black storm cloud rising from between the two men, a dark, roiling mass that spread out into the room and became… crows! Hundreds of them! Flapping, shrieking, their wings beating against the walls, their claws reaching out, their sharp grey beaks and bright black eyes everywhere she turned.

Dora ducked in terror, as a cloud of blackness hurtled towards her. She put her arms up over her face, and curled into a tight ball on the ground, but she could feel them pecking, clawing, beating at her back, and sharp pincers pulling at her hair.

There were yells and crashes all around but she didn't dare look, in case they pecked at her eyes. She curled tighter, and buried her face in her knees. She could hardly breathe.

Just as she thought she might pass out, there was a great commotion just next to her, a mixture of shouts and bangs and the shrieks of birds. She felt a great heavy cloth sweep across her, beating the birds back, and then it was thrown right over her like a blanket and she found herself safe, in a kind of protective tent. The birds were still pecking and jabbing, but the cloth was thick, and they weren't getting through. Close by, in the dimness, she could see Jem on his hands and knees, breathing heavily. His face was pale, and there was rather a lot of blood on it.

"I couldn't think what to do," he panted. "And then I noticed that there were these huge tapestries over the windows, so I cut one down with my sword. I thought if I got it over you, kept the birds off, you might be able to do some magic."

Dora could feel the crows, beating themselves angrily against the heavy cloth, and hear shrieks and the sounds of falling furniture around them.

The cold magic that had come from Smith and Jones seemed to be seeping into her bones. She wasn't sure she would be able to do anything, but she took a deep breath and nodded.

"Lift the edge of the cloth," she said. "I need to see what's happening."

Jem lifted up one corner a little, and they both peered out. One of the old ladies, nearby, had three crows in her hair, while her friend was cursing loudly and trying to beat them away with a cushion. Simon was deep in a swirl of blackness, hacking wildly at the birds with the sword, which he'd managed to wrestle free of its bin bag. Cat was cowering on the ground with her hands over her head, while Sir Bedwyr stood above her, cutting down crow after crow with his bright sword. He had been raked by several beaks and claws, and blood was running down his face. Albert Jemmet was surrounded by birds, but his strange contraption was obviously doing something, as crows were turning to white dust all around him, so much so that he looked like a man caught in a snowstorm. But more and more birds continued to come.

And then Dora saw something that made her

clutch Jem very tightly. Stalking towards Albert, through another whirl of crows, were the two dark-suited figures of Mr Smith and Mr Jones.

"Go on, Dora!" urged Jem, thumping her on the arm. "You can do it – I know you can! You've got really strong magic. Turn them small or something!"

He grinned at her, and wiped a trickle of blood away from his eye. Dora gave him a shaky grin in return and raised her arms. Concentrating on the two figures approaching Albert, she started to mutter the words of an immobility spell.

The coldness was rising around her as Smith and Jones got nearer, and it was making it hard to reach for her magic, hard to gather it together into the spell. Dora fought against the iciness seeping into her bones, drew on every bit of power she could raise up, and threw the spell straight at their heads.

Simon kept inhaling crows' feathers. He was spitting them out, whirling the sword around his head as wildly as he could and trying very hard to see where Smith and Jones were, when suddenly he heard a shout from Cat. He jerked his head round in time to see Sir Bedwyr, assaulted by at least ten crows at once, go toppling backwards into Albert Jemmet. Albert's fumigator flew out of his hands and crashed into the widescreen TV in the corner of the residents' lounge. Smith and Jones, Simon saw with horror, were just a few steps away. As he saw Albert stagger, Mr Jones gave a snarl and lunged forward.

But at that very moment there was a sound like the chiming of a bell. Everything seemed to slow down, and Simon could hear nothing but ringing in his ears. As it gradually faded away, he blinked, and realised that the crows had gone – every single one. Smith and Jones were frozen like statues in the centre of the room, and Albert and Sir Bedwyr were slowly untangling themselves and getting up off the floor.

A heap of red velvet curtain down by the sofa bulged surprisingly, and from it emerged Jem, pulling Dora behind him. Jem looked rather the worse for wear, and Dora was very pale, but Albert reached down and helped pull her to her feet with a grin.

"That was you, was it, that immobility spell?" he said cheerily. "You nearly got all of us, there.

My ears are still ringing! Not that I'm complaining. That came just in the nick of time, I can tell you… Smith *or* Jones I could have dealt with, but the two of them together had put a hex on me so strong I couldn't have magicked a teaspoon out of a cutlery drawer. All I had left was my trusty fumigator." He looked around for it, and spotted it by the TV, rather bent out of shape. "Ah well," he said, picking it up gently. "Looks like it needs a bit of tender loving care."

Sir Bedwyr, breathing heavily and mopping the blood from his face with a convenient cushion, reached down to pull Cat to her feet.

"Th- thanks," she said, rather shakily. "For… protecting me."

Sir Bedwyr straightened his shoulders and looked distinctly pleased with himself. "Always glad to be of service to a beauteous damsel!" he said, with a bow.

Simon was looking at the immobilised figures of Smith and Jones. They were completely still, but there was something in the depths of their black eyes that made him sure they were aware of everything. He shivered.

"Will they… stay like that now?" he said.

"And what happened to the crows?"

"The crows were their magic," said Albert. "Can't do magic when you're immobilised. But as for how long they'll stay like that..." He came over and had a good look. "I'd say not too long, actually – it might be a good idea if we scarpered sharpish."

"Oh, I'd say that would indeed be a good idea," came a drawling voice from the other end of the room. "But I'm not inclined to let you go."

Dora turned towards the voice, and her breath caught in her throat. Because surveying the room with an air of interest, while lazily shaking out the lace cuffs of his velvet sleeves, was the tall, dark figure of Lord Ravenglass.

Chapter Eighteen

Lord Ravenglass waved one hand lazily at the residents of Sunset Court, who were looking extremely dishevelled and rather bemused. Suddenly they all acquired a glazed expression, and bowed deeply. He beckoned them towards the hallway and gradually they sidled out of the room with their shovels and lampstands, looking sheepish and muttering about teatime. The door closed behind them with a firm bang.

"Dear me," said Lord Ravenglass, flicking an imaginary piece of dust off his velvet sleeve and smiling at Albert Jemmet. "I seem to have got here just in time. I was hoping to avoid having to come myself, but..." he shrugged, "alas, incompetence surrounds me."

Simon glanced at Albert, who was looking

distinctly uneasy at the appearance of this smoothly dressed man, with his velvet and lace and long black ringlets. However, Jemmet stepped forward smartly, and bowed very low.

"Albert Jemmet, your Lordship," he said. "Agent for the Great Forest, currently attached to this world. We've been having a bit of trouble with these two... vermin," he gestured at the frozen figures of Smith and Jones, "but I believe we have the situation under control."

"Indeed?" said Lord Ravenglass, flashing a gleaming smile at everyone. "Dora... *and* Jem. Glad to see you're here as well. On the case, eh?" He winked at Jem, who bowed with a flourish. Dora, Simon noticed, bowed with altogether less enthusiasm.

Lord Ravenglass moved forward regally, then halted and put his face up very close to Albert's.

"The amber, Jemmet," he said softly. "I require the amber."

Albert Jemmet's blue eyes met Lord Ravenglass's gaze firmly. Simon held his breath. After a pause, Albert said, in a very neutral voice, "I don't have it, your Lordship. I'm sorry."

Cat caught Simon's eye, and he flicked his

gaze towards the door. She gave the tiniest of nods and started to sidle away. As she did so, Sir Bedwyr moved forward, bowed low to Lord Ravenglass and started to explain about his quest, and offer his services to find whatever it was that his Lordship wanted – but Ravenglass just held up one white hand with a frown and Sir Bedwyr stuttered into silence.

There was a pause, while Lord Ravenglass examined Albert Jemmet as if he were fitting him for a coffin. Then he snapped his fingers.

"I had hoped to avoid this," he said. "But maybe I shall need Smith and Jones after all." He lightly touched the two frozen figures standing nearby, and they stirred and looked around. Moving stiffly, as if still not quite free of Dora's spell, they placed themselves either side of Lord Ravenglass and stood ready, their black eyes sweeping the room.

"Ah," said Albert. "They're working for you, then."

Lord Ravenglass smiled. "As you say. They are working for me." He raised his voice. "The amber is in this room, and if it's not handed over *at once*, I'll be asking my trusty friends here to find it. And," he examined his fingernails lazily, "while they may not have completely recovered their powers, you can be sure that they *won't* be asking politely." He beamed round at them all, then raised one eyebrow at Jem. "Any ideas, Jem?" he asked. "Before I let them loose?"

Jem looked at Lord Ravenglass and thought about the knighthood he had been promised. He thought about lording it over all the useless stuck-up squires at Roland Castle and being right-hand man to the heir to the throne. But then he thought about Smith and Jones and the crows that had attacked them all. They were *working for* Lord Ravenglass. He shivered, and thought about Lord Ravenglass's shiny, too-white teeth when he smiled, and his haughty insistence that everyone bow to him at exactly forty-five degrees to the horizontal. He glanced at Dora, and she shook her head sternly.

He shrugged. "We haven't managed to find it, your Lordship," he said apologetically. "I have no idea where it is."

Visibly irritated, Lord Ravenglass gestured to Smith and Jones and the two of them nodded. Mr Smith stalked towards Dora. He pinched her shoulder hard, and shook her till her teeth rattled. Jem kicked him on the shins but he simply reached out one hand, grabbed Jem by the back of his jerkin and hauled him, yelling, off his feet. Mr Jones headed straight for Cat, who was now pelting for the door of the lounge. As he reached for her, Sir Bedwyr swung his long sword into Mr Jones's back, and Albert brought the fumigator crashing down on his head – but Mr Jones hardly seemed to notice. He wrenched Cat's rucksack off her back, and pulled it in half with a tearing, splitting sound. The contents went flying, and the wooden box with the amber tumbled across the floor and came to a halt on the thick Persian rug in the middle of the lounge.

Lord Ravenglass raised one eyebrow.

"Well, well," he said. "I rather thought so. That'll be the box with the deep amber. *Just* what I've been looking for."

"It's not yours," said Albert swiftly. "You don't need it anyway. You'll inherit the queen's piece."

Lord Ravenglass looked up at the ceiling, with an air of mock patience. "That mad old witch," he said, "refuses to die, or give the amber up. For now. And besides," he smiled round, showing all of his white teeth, "I find I need more than one piece. So I'll be taking this one."

He clicked his fingers, and the box burst into flames, then crackled with ice, and then released a tornado of wind which ruffled through Lord Ravenglass's ringlets. The amber jewel rolled out into the middle of the rug.

There was a pause, while they all looked at it. Then Lord Ravenglass started to move towards the centre of the room. At once Great-Aunt Irene materialised above the discarded box, her silvery outline becoming rapidly solid, and her cane waving wildly in the direction of the advancing figure. She cried out in a very loud voice: "I can't do anything! I'm a ghost! I can't use magic! It's no good waiting for Louis any longer – someone else is going to have to do it! Simon – Cat – you're both heirs! Will one of you for goodness sake PICK UP THE AMBER BEFORE HE GETS IT!"

Simon and Cat looked across at each other, shocked. They were both about the same distance from the amber – but Lord Ravenglass was closer. Neither of them were going to get the amber unless someone stopped or slowed Lord Ravenglass. There was a split second to make a decision, but Simon knew immediately what he had to do. He was closest to Lord Ravenglass, and he had the sword.

"Cat! Take it!" he shouted, and lunged at Lord Ravenglass, smacking the sword into the back of his long elegant legs.

"Ow!" yelled Lord Ravenglass in an extremely undignified manner, and stumbled onto his hands and knees. His long white fingers stretched out desperately towards the amber but Cat was quicker. She stamped on his hand and kicked the amber out of reach. The jewel was glowing fiercely, and it looked incredibly hot. Cat could distinctly remember Jem's scorched fingers after he had picked it up in the kitchen, but Lord Ravenglass was starting to get up, and she was now much closer to the jewel than Simon. Closing her eyes, and praying that the amber would not burn her, she bent down, closed her fingers round it, and stood up, holding it firmly in her hand.

There was a sudden stillness. She could see the orange stone glowing between her fingers, and feel the jangling energy from it almost numbing her arm, but her fingers were not even hot. As she continued to hold it, the glow gradually faded, and the energy crackling outwards from it started to become smoother and calmer. The silence around them suddenly had a different quality to it – as if a constant low hum that they'd barely noticed had disappeared.

"That's better," said Albert. "Can hear myself think at last."

Great-Aunt Irene clapped her hands.

"Well done, my dear!" she said. "Jolly well done! It's yours now, you know. You're the new heir."

She turned to Lord Ravenglass, who had picked himself up off the floor and was looking utterly furious.

"*So* sorry," she said brightly. "It looks like you've failed. The amber has passed on. So if you could just…" she waved her hands vaguely at Mr Smith and Mr Jones, "you know, get off home. That would be wonderful. And give my regards to your aunt. Irene Morgan – we're sixth cousins or something similar, I believe."

"Sixth cousins, eh?" said Lord Ravenglass, through gritted teeth. "Well, it doesn't really matter. Because as far as I can see, you're still a ghost, and these… *children* don't seem up to much. So I do believe if it came to a magical fight, it would be myself and my very able companions against the dubious powers of Albert and young Dora here. I suggest," he grinned at them, "you see sense now and hand that amber over to me."

Dora struggled to free herself from Mr Smith's claw-like grip, and Jem yelled and pulled, but neither of them could get away. Mr Jones anticipated a move from Sir Bedwyr, and brought him crashing down on the carpet with a well-placed foot and a shove, then turned to Jemmet. The two of them watched each other warily. Simon tried to dodge past to get to Dora, but Lord Ravenglass reached out a lazy hand and stopped him in his tracks. Simon felt as if his feet had been turned to blocks of stone. He looked helplessly at Cat, who had gone very white.

"Use the amber," said Great-Aunt Irene calmly to Cat. "Just tell it what to do. Send them back to where they came from."

Cat's head ached, and she could feel her hand trembling. Only a few days ago the whole idea of magic had seemed like make-believe. And yet now here it was, all around her – magic, rifts, other worlds. It was real. And now it was up to her to control the jewel's power. Somehow she had to draw on some part of her, deep down, that knew about magic, that had always known about it.

Cat looked at Lord Ravenglass, and she saw a flicker in his eyes as he glanced from her to the amber. He's afraid, she thought. He knows I could do it. She clenched the amber tightly, and wondered how. How was she supposed to use it? Just tell it, Great-Aunt Irene had said. Just tell it what to do.

"G-go b-back!" Cat said loudly, holding the amber out in front of her. "Lord Ravenglass. And Mr Smith. Mr Jones. Go back to wherever you came from! I… I command you!"

A whirling white mist rose in front of her, and it reached out little tendrils towards Lord Ravenglass, and then Smith and Jones. Mr Smith cursed, and let go of Dora and Jem. Mr Jones gave a rasping snarl, and started to run, but the two of them were pulled into the mist in one short blink, and then gone.

Lord Ravenglass raised his eyes to the ceiling. "Damn," he said. And then he was gone too.

At that moment, the doors at the other end of

the lounge opened, and a tall lanky figure ran in, wearing a railway inspector's jacket and looking rather out of breath.

"Did you manage to shut down the amber? Am I too late? There was a points failure. I got stuck at Clapham Junction for an *hour*."

Chapter Nineteen

"It's the Druid!" shouted Dora, in a glad voice.

"Louis Henry Maximillian Morgan!" As she spoke, Great-Aunt Irene picked up a small jug from a nearby table and hurled it across the room. The Druid ducked, and it crashed against the wall just behind his head.

"Er... hello, Mother," he said, rather sheepishly. "Sorry I couldn't come to the funeral. You're looking... very smart and... er... silvery." He looked across at Simon and Cat.

"Uncle Lou!" said Cat, feeling a sudden gladness at the sight of him. "But... What...? How...?"

"Lovely to see you again," he said with a warm smile. "It's been such a long time. Last time I was in this world, you were both small enough to sit on my knee. And here you are now, so grown-up!"

"*You good-for-nothing irresponsible wastrel!*" Great-Aunt Irene shouted at him, her anger making her turn alternately solid and transparent. "You're too late! Where have you *been*? How could you be so utterly useless? You – you –" she almost choked, trying to decide what to say next, and the Druid seized his chance. Moving swiftly to the centre of the room, and with a quick grin at Dora and Jem, he put out his hands towards his mother and made soothing gestures.

"I'm sorry," he said. "I should have come earlier. But I promised not to interfere. I was hoping someone else..." He spread his hands apologetically. "I made sure the queen knew. I thought Ravenglass would deal with it."

"He nearly did," said Albert dryly. "But it seems he wanted the amber for himself, so it's lucky that Cat here got there first."

The Druid looked taken aback. "Ah," he said. "Well. That puts a different complexion on it." He glanced round at the room, with its upturned chairs and battered bits of furniture. "Maybe we'd better all have a bit of a chat. I'll put a very strong 'Do not disturb' spell on the room, and get us some refreshments."

The Druid, with a little bit of charm and a slight dose of magic, managed to persuade the matron to provide them with a magnificent tea. Mrs Allsop was rather confused about everything that had happened, but somehow ended up with the impression that the Druid and his colleagues had been responsible for defusing some kind of bomb on the premises. She was extremely grateful, and quite happy to provide tea, cake and buns in return for their efforts, while she busied herself sorting out the rest of the residents and letting the staff out of the meeting room.

Cat was still feeling rather weak, and she gladly accepted a mug of tea with six sugars from Albert Jemmet, who gave her a friendly smile.

"Bit of a shock, I imagine," he said, nodding to the amber, which was now hanging round her neck on its bronze chain.

She reached up and touched it. "I had no idea," she said. "But now… it somehow feels exactly right."

He nodded. "Funny really," he said. "Because I thought it was young Simon that was going to be the one. But he seems happy enough with the sword."

Cat looked over at Simon, with the sword resting on his lap, and grinned. "He really needs to learn how to use it properly, though," she said. "He massacred Mum's sofa last time he tried. And cut up most of her washing."

Simon looked up as he felt Cat's eyes on him, and waved. He was grilling Dora on magic. "So, do you think you could show me some stuff? Just small things. I think I might be able to do it, and I'd really like to know how."

Dora looked at him and considered. He clearly did have magic, she could sense it bubbling away inside him. But magic was not really part of this world, and she was pretty sure the Druid would not approve of her showing him how to use it. She glanced down to the other end of the room, where the Druid was deep in conversation with Great-Aunt Irene. Then she checked to her right, where Sir Bedwyr was cheerfully tucking into a plate of cream buns and polishing his sword with a bit of torn curtain.

Dora knew she should say no, but part of her was starting to get a bit fed up of always worrying about what she was *supposed* to do. Jem never did anything except what he wanted to, and he seemed to get away with it. And Dora realised that she rather *wanted* to help Simon awaken his magic properly, and show him just what a fantastic thing it was.

"Okay," she said to Simon, with a quick nod. "Just a bit. But don't tell anyone I showed you. They'd probably make me muck the pigs out for a whole year."

She gestured to him to slip behind the large overstuffed sofa, where they would be out of sight. Jem noticed them go, but didn't say anything. He had a bakewell tart in one hand and a buttered roll in the other, and was rapidly demolishing them both. He was also rather busy trying to question Albert Jemmet about deep amber and the forest and the other worlds.

"So," he said, gesturing with the remains of the bakewell tart. "There are lots of worlds, and they all originate in the Great Forest. That's what Caractacus told us. But the world with the kingdom is the *real* one. Our world."

"Well, they're all real," said Albert. "And they all contain a part of the forest, somewhere. But yes, the kingdom is the first. It's where the World Tree has its roots."

"And the forest agents are the ones that look after all the worlds," said Jem. "Can anyone become one? Even a commoner?"

Albert looked at Jem's eager expression and grinned. "Yes – why, do you want to try for the job?"

Jem's eyes sparkled. "I might think about it," he said, airily. "So – what about this deep amber? How can it make stuff – people – go from one world to another?"

"The amber... Well..." said Albert, "that's not really for just anyone to know about. It's old, it's part of the World Tree. It has some of the tree's power. That means you can use it to move between the worlds, among other things. The amber has always belonged to the heirs of the kingdom, and they've generally worked with the forest to help keep the worlds balanced."

"So, Cat's an heir," said Jem, trying to get it straight in his head. "But Lord Ravenglass is an heir too, isn't he? He gets the queen's amber. So are there other pieces, and other heirs?"

"Yes," said the Druid, turning as he heard Jem's question. "There were four bits originally, but they got scattered throughout the worlds. Lost.

Each heir to the amber knew where their bit was, but not the others. And of course, some heirs didn't even know they *were* heirs." He looked over at Cat, apologetically.

Cat slurped her tea, and looked back at him. The six sugars had revived her, and she was beginning to feel that there were some people who had rather a lot of explaining to do. She pointed her teaspoon at the Druid with a frown. "Why didn't you *tell* us? And why did you just disappear?"

The Druid looked slightly sheepish.

"You were rather young when I left," he said. "And I had no idea things would get this out of hand."

"So if I'm an heir, and Simon is as well, does that mean Dad was too?" she asked.

He nodded, and leaned back in his chair, stretching his long legs out in front of him. "We grew up together," he said. "In the kingdom. But we did a lot of travelling between worlds, one way and another. Got into a fair few scrapes..." He grinned, as if remembering some of them.

Great-Aunt Irene snorted. "Your father and Louis were a terrible pair. They got into all sorts of trouble, in the kingdom and other worlds. I never knew from one day to the next where they'd be. But then they decided to settle down here, of all places. So here is where I came as well, to keep an eye on them."

"It was so peaceful in this world," said the Druid, dreamily. "No magic, and there were chocolate fudge sundaes and hot water and trains and electrical gadgets... And then your dad met Florence, and they got married and had you. It was all rather lovely. Until the accident." He stopped, and ran his hands through his hair, and shrugged. "It was very difficult for a while, after that. I tried to help. And then... well, I had a terrible row with your mother, and she said she never wanted to see me again. I shouldn't really be here now."

"What was the row about?" said Cat.

"I – well... I– I can't say. You'll have to ask her."

There was a pause, and the Druid looked rather miserable.

"What I'd like to know, though," said Jem, changing the subject swiftly, "is what Lord Ravenglass is up to."

"I think we'd all like to know that," said Albert, grimly.

The Druid exchanged glances with Great-Aunt Irene.

"Yes," he said. "Well. It's something we've just been discussing. The thing is, I can't see any reason for him wanting this amber for himself unless he's thinking of gathering all four pieces. Remaking the crown."

Albert choked on his cup of tea and had to be thumped on the back by Jem.

"Remaking the crown?" he spluttered. "After all these years?"

"I think so," said the Druid. "It would explain a lot of things that have been happening in the kingdom recently. Since he took over as Regent, there have been very bad relations with the forest. And he's always been rather ambitious."

"Sorry," said Cat. "But what's the crown? And what would it matter if he did remake it?"

Albert picked up the sugar bowl, and spooned an extra three sugars into his mug. Then he added three more for good measure.

"It's an ancient crown of the kingdom," he said, taking a slurp. "The story is, that in the far, far past, the creatures of the dark gained in power. The king at the time, Bruni, had a half-brother, who was part-human, part-wolf, and a shape-shifter. This half-brother, Lukas, joined forces with the dark, and he became known as the Lord of the Wolves. He threatened all the worlds – not just the kingdom. To fight him, the king forged a magical sword, and he used it to cut into the World Tree, east, west, north and south. Four tears of amber sap dripped from the tree, and when they hardened, he forged an iron crown to hold them. With the sword, and the crown, he beat back the creatures of darkness and imprisoned the Lord of Wolves. But the crown was too powerful and dangerous to keep in one piece – so Bruni's four heirs took a piece of amber each. One stayed to rule the kingdom, and the others took their pieces across the worlds to new realms. But over the generations, they got scattered, and the bits of amber were lost... No one knew who had them. Except for the one in the kingdom, of course. That's the piece Queen Igraine has now. The thing is – with all four pieces, with the whole crown remade, there'd be no one who could stand against its bearer, not even in the forest. The person who had the crown would rule not just the kingdom but the World Tree and all the worlds in it. They would have the power to destroy all of them if they chose."

"Lord Ravenglass," said Great-Aunt Irene with immense dislike. "He always struck me as a nasty piece of work. He's got to be stopped before he does something… regrettable."

"Well, he can't have this piece," said Cat firmly, holding the amber in her hand.

"No," said the Druid, cheerfully. "And it was very well done, taking it before he got a chance. But he'll be after it again, there's no doubt of that. And besides, one piece is not going to be enough. If he manages to get the others we won't be able to hold him off for long."

"Well then," said Jem. "We'll just have to find the other bits before he does. Does anyone know where to start looking?"

But just then, there was a loud bang from behind the sofa and Simon and Dora scrambled out looking slightly singed. A plume of grey smoke shot up to the ceiling, and a few sparks whizzed across the room before burning themselves out on the Persian rug. Sir Bedwyr had his hand on his sword and was looking round rather wildly.

The Druid looked at Dora with one eyebrow raised.

"Um – sorry," she said, but she was clearly stifling a bad case of the giggles. "Accident with a shrinking spell."

"Shrinking spell?" said Jem, in mock horror. "You don't want to let Dora anywhere near you with a shrinking spell! She tried that on me in the forest, and then she couldn't turn me back."

"It's okay," said Simon, rubbing soot out of his eyes. "It's under control. So – what were you all talking about?"

"We were talking," said the Druid briskly, "about how to get you all back home. And Albert and I will need to consult with a few others – try to decide what to do about Ravenglass. He's still the queen's nephew, and he's still in charge of the kingdom. We're going to have to be very, very careful."

Chapter Twenty

A fine drizzle of rain was falling on the garden of Sunset Court as they emerged from the main door. The Druid looked up and adjusted the collar of his jacket.

"Always raining in this world," he said cheerfully.

They had just been chased out of the lounge by the matron, who had a queue of residents waiting to watch the TV.

As they walked away from the house, Dappletoes, who'd been patiently waiting outside, eating the pot plants, trotted up to them happily and nudged Sir Bedwyr. The knight stroked his horse's nose fondly.

"So," said the Druid, looking for a suitable place to conjure a portal. "I think it's time to get

Sir Bedwyr and the rest of the rabble back to the castle, eh Albert?"

"Rabble?" said Jem. "Do you mean us?"

"You and Dora, yes," said the Druid. "Much as I'd like to leave you in an entirely different world, Jem, Sir Mortimer is very keen to talk to you. Something to do with the squires' undergarments."

"The lads did it, then?" said Jem, looking delighted. "Brilliant! Although... um... I have no idea what you're talking about, you know. Did you say undergarments?"

Dora laughed. She was surprised to find that she was quite looking forward to getting back to the castle and a bit of normality. And after coping with several days of Jem, to say nothing of other worlds, magic battles and general mayhem, she had a feeling she wouldn't be quite so worried about Violet Wetherby and her bunch of cronies any more. She grinned at Jem, and then turned to Simon.

"Good luck!" she said, with a meaningful look.

Simon raised his sword, wrapped back up carefully in its towel and bin bag, and gave her a wink. "See you soon!" he said.

"Or not," said the Druid, giving Simon a hard stare. "I'm leaving you the sword, Simon, because it was your dad's. It seems right that you should have it. But I really hope you're not planning any kind of attempt at portal magic with it. Because that would be exceedingly unwise."

Simon met the Druid's brown eyes steadily.

"Of course not," he said, with his most innocent expression. The Druid held his gaze for a moment, and then turned away.

"Albert?" he said. "Are you with me?"

Albert Jemmet hooked his thumbs into the belt loops of his blue overalls, and nodded.

"Yes," he said firmly. "I'll come to Roland Castle first, then get my report to the forest. We can get a few people together and make plans."

"But what about us?" said Cat, waving at herself and Simon and the ghostly outline of Great-Aunt Irene. "Aren't we going to help? What are we supposed to do? What do we tell Mum?"

"Nothing," said the Druid swiftly. "Nothing at all. It's probably best if you don't even mention you've seen me, in fact. You mother... um... I don't think she'd be very happy about it."

He didn't look very happy about it himself, but he tried to give Cat and Simon a cheerful smile. "I'll be back – when we've sorted out a few things. But Florence would really never forgive me if I let you get involved in all this. I need you to stay here and stay safe."

He looked across at Great-Aunt Irene. "Mother?" he said, meaningfully.

Great-Aunt Irene looked rather mutinous.

"The amber has passed on," said the Druid, firmly.

"I know, I know. Time for me to go," said Great-Aunt Irene. She gestured to the Druid to bend down, and planted a silvery kiss on his forehead. "Be good," she said. "Look after them all."

She unclasped a small silver locket from around her neck, then turned to Cat. "Here you are, my dear," she said, and put it into Cat's hand. As she did so, the locket turned quite solid. "I have to go, really – but I don't like to leave you completely with so much going on. So, I'll just fold myself up into the locket for now – if you need me, just open it."

She started to shimmer, and become more transparent. When she seemed to be no more than a collection of silvery dust, the dust gathered itself together and whooshed into the silver locket, and then Great-Aunt Irene was gone.

For a moment, the Druid continued to look at the place where she'd been, then he shook himself and clapped his hands. "Come on then," he said. "Better get on with it. I've got the key to my room somewhere, should be able to conjure a portal back with that..." He rummaged around in his clothes, shrugging off the railway inspector's jacket as he did so.

"Umm – we've got a silver cup Lord Ravenglass gave us," said Dora, offering it to him. "For getting back."

Albert gave a wry grin. "I don't think so," he said. "That would take us back to Lord Ravenglass's apartments – which is probably the last place we want to be arriving just now."

"Ah, got it!" said the Druid triumphantly, holding up a rather battered metal key. He made a complicated series of hand gestures over it, and a misty portal appeared between two rose bushes.

"Sir Bedwyr?" he said, gesturing to the knight.

Dappletoes trotted eagerly towards the white

mist, and as he did so Sir Bedwyr threw himself into the saddle and raised his sword in salute at them all.

"Farewell! May we meet again on another such fascinating quest!"

"Not if I can help it," muttered Albert darkly, and Simon laughed.

"Jem?" said the Druid. "Dora?"

Jem thumped Simon on the back and bowed to Cat with a flourish that made her giggle. Dora turned rather pink and gave them both a big hug.

Albert came over and shook Simon's hand, and then smiled at Cat.

"Keep the amber safe," he said. "And don't worry, you'll be safe enough here while we sort out Lord Ravenglass and his nasty chums." Then he patted her on the back, nodded at Simon, and walked through the portal. Jem and Dora waved and walked after him.

The Druid looked across at Cat, and gave her a grin. "You know, the amber's gone to a much more deserving heir than me. I'll be back – and in the meantime, don't get into trouble, either of you. And *don't* say anything to your mother!"

He gave them a cheery wave, and disappeared

into the mist, and the mist immediately winked out of existence. There were just the two rose bushes, and gradually darkening twilight, and the long driveway leading out of the grounds.

"Well," said Cat, after a moment. "I guess we'd better get home."

They turned for the driveway and started walking slowly away from Sunset Court.

"So, is that it then?" said Simon, swinging the sword in its towel and bin bag as they emerged out onto the road. "Are we just supposed to wait for Uncle Lou to come back and get us when it's all safe?"

Cat raised her eyebrows at Simon.

"Why?" she said. "Do you have an alternative?"

He grinned.

"I might, as it happens," he said. "When we were behind the sofa, Dora taught me how to make a portal spell. I didn't get it quite right – but I was watching Uncle Lou carefully just now. I reckon with a bit of practice I might be able to use the sword to get us to the kingdom. I don't see why we should be left out of it all!"

Cat laughed. "I thought you had something up your sleeve," she said. "But if that doesn't work, we might have another way in. Albert Jemmet said you can use the amber to get to any world you want to."

"Really?" said Simon his eyes sparkling. "Did he explain how?"

"No," said Cat. "But it seems to work just by telling it what you want. It should be quite simple."

Simon thought about the Druid's words to them. "Stay here, and stay safe." But then he thought about the dusty black figures of Mr Smith and Mr Jones, and Lord Ravenglass with his velvet and lace and his lazy drawl. They would be trying to find the remaining bits of amber, and it was clear that the simplest way to stop them was to get there first. That was what the Druid and Albert would be planning, and possibly Dora and Jem would be roped in to help. Simon was absolutely determined not to be left out.

He thought about all that had happened to them over the last few days – magic, and ghosts, and shining swords appearing from nowhere. The kingdom. His dad had known about the kingdom, he'd been there, he'd learnt to use his sword there. Simon could feel the sword, wrapped in its layers of towel and bin bag, still gently humming with power, and he grinned. He could feel a bubble of excitement building inside him at the thought that this other world was part of who he was. There was no way he was going to sit around and wait till Uncle Lou came back to collect them.

When they finally got home, rather tired and full of plans, they found their mum sitting at the kitchen table, looking over some old manuscripts with a cup of coffee in her hand. She looked up and smiled at them, waving at the cooker behind her.

"Pasta in the saucepan, apple crumble in the oven – help yourselves," she said, and then she pointed her pen at Simon sternly. "And when you've eaten, you can explain to me exactly what you did to the sofa, and my washing."

Epilogue

The white stone walls of the palace were humming with the extreme displeasure of the queen's nephew and heir, Lord Ravenglass. Servants were scurrying back and forth, heads lowered, ready at a moment's notice to bow to the exact degree necessary for a third-level courtier, or a second-level nobleman, or even – Forest forbid – the exact forty-five degrees necessary to appease Lord Ravenglass himself.

Ollie Bowbuckle, fourth apprentice under-footman, was in the deepest part of the cellars, cowering behind a heavy wooden door. He had been sent down to fetch up a morsel of his Lordship's favourite oak-smoked vintage cheese. His Lordship's manservant had ordered it, in the hope that an array of tempting trifles would distract Lord Ravenglass from his current pursuit of blasting the towers of the east wing with bolts of were-lightning. The damage to the gargoyles already looked like being the worst since Queen Igraine had refused to abdicate in her nephew's favour two years previously.

Ollie, a rather skinny, fair-haired lad of fourteen, had never been down to the under-cellars before, but he'd been the only one they could spare when the message came to the kitchens. Butterworth, the chief under-footman, had sent him down with strict instructions to get the cheese in double-quick time or he'd be on latrine duty for a week. And now Ollie was completely lost. He would have happily spent seven days scrubbing the palace sewers in exchange for being shown the way out.

He'd taken a wrong turn, he knew that now. Instead of the cheese pantry, he'd ended up in a warren of dark, damp passages, and behind every door was just another passage, or stone steps winding downwards, or an empty stone chamber. And then, halfway across one of the badly lit chambers, he'd walked into some kind of invisible wall. Beyond it there was a faint blue glow, and what appeared to be the outline of a cave, but he could see very little else. Until he had backed away, and slipped on the dank stone floor, and cried out as he fell. All at once a dark shadow had stirred at the edge of the cave, and Ollie had seen that it was a man – gaunt, his skin pale and almost tinged blue, his eyes desperate.

"Who's there?" the man had called, in a rasping voice, peering towards where Ollie lay. He had moved forward then, slowly, and Ollie had realised with a shock that he had heavy silver chains on his legs and arms.

"Show yourself!" the man had cried, but Ollie, trembling, had eased himself backwards across the floor until he reached the sturdy oak door through which he'd entered. And that was when he heard the sound of footsteps coming down the narrow, winding stairs beyond the door. Ollie swallowed, and pressed himself into the shadows.

There were many secrets buried within the white walls of Queen Igraine's palace, and servants learned early on to keep their eyes on the job and their curiosity under check, or else they might just become one of those buried secrets themselves. Something told Ollie that he was in a place where apprentice under-footmen were not expected to be, and it might be better not to be discovered there.

As he held his breath, the person who had been coming down the stairs walked into the chamber. Ollie nearly fainted from terror. The man who had emerged from the doorway, in a flash of white lace and dark curls, was the queen's nephew, Lord Ravenglass, and he was not in a good mood.

Lord Ravenglass stalked up to where Ollie had hit the invisible wall and snapped his fingers at the man in chains.

"Lost!" he said, his voice thick with anger. "Slipped through my fingers! I was *this* close!"

He held up his thumb and forefinger, almost touching. The man in chains looked up hungrily. His fair hair was lank and dirty, and he was painfully thin, but he somehow still had an air of being powerful, dangerous – like a caged animal.

"The amber?" he said, his blue eyes strangely bright.

"Yes, the amber," said Lord Ravenglass irritably. "Almost in my grasp. And then it was taken from me by a slip of a girl – barely thirteen.

Albert Jemmet was there. Meddling as usual."

Lord Ravenglass started pacing up and down in front of the invisible wall, his fingers twitching from rage, his eyes focused on the prisoner beyond. Now was Ollie's best chance to leave. Barely breathing, he started to ease himself around the door, as Lord Ravenglass was speaking.

"I did some digging when I came back. Irene Morgan, she said she was, the meddlesome old woman who owned it before. Which makes the girl who took it Catrin Arnold. She's got a brother – Simon. But they're under the Forest's protection now. I won't be able to get at them. Not till we've got more power."

"Irene Morgan…" said the man in chains, slowly. It was as if he were tasting the name, savouring it. "And Catrin Arnold…"

Lord Ravenglass stopped, and raised his eyebrows. "You have an idea?"

The man stood up, grimacing with pain as he stretched his limbs.

"I think we can get Catrin and her brother to help us," he said, and gave Lord Ravenglass a twisted smile. "The Forest can't protect them if they choose to come to us of their own accord."

Lord Ravenglass frowned. "And why should they do that?"

As Ollie backed away into the passageway, the last thing he heard was the prisoner's reply.

"Because they'll come when you tell them you need the amber to release me. To release their father."

Coming soon...

DRAGON AMBER

Simon and Cat are determined to find their way
to the kingdom – but it soon becomes more
dangerous than they could have imagined.

Meanwhile, the Druid is keeping secrets from
Dora and Jem. Should they try and follow him
to the mysterious Empire of Akkad, where
there might be dragons…?

Join the fearless foursome once more as they
race to track down the next piece of amber.